WELSH FOL   S

ROBIN GWYNDAF

Robin Gwyndaf

ILLUSTRATED BY MARGARET D. JONES

2024

Front cover illustration:

Adar Llyn Syfaddan, Sir Frycheiniog, yn canu'n uchel,
yng ngwydd dau Arglwydd Normanaidd, i ddatgan mai
Gruffudd ap Rhys oedd gwir Dywysog Deheubarth Cymru.

The Birds of Llyn Syfaddan (Llan-gors), Brecknockshire,
in the company of two Norman Lords, singing loudly to
proclaim Gruffudd ap Rhys the true Prince of South Wales.

First edition: 1989
Revised 5th edition: 2024

ISBN: 978-1-80099-532-1

Printed and published in Wales
on paper from sustainable forests by
Y Lolfa Cyf., Talybont, Ceredigion SY24 5HE
e-mail ylolfa@ylolfa.com
website www.ylolfa.com
phone 01970 832 304
fax 01970 832 782

Contents

'Yntau, Wydion, gorau cyfarwydd yn y byd ydoedd.'
('And he, Gwydion, was the best storyteller in the world.')
Fourth Branch of the Mabinogi. Second half of the 11th century.

◆

Countryman: 'We old men are old chronicles, and when our tongues go they are not clocks to tell only the time present, but large books unclasped; and our speeches, like leaves turned over and over, discover wonders that are long past.'
17th century tract.

◆

'The old house, cowshed and barn were all under one roof, a long, low building. The cowshed was nearest the kitchen with only a wooden partition separating them, and the sound of the cattle scraping their horns, the milking and the munching could clearly be heard from the kitchen. There was a large oak threshold at the bottom of each door from the kitchen to the barn. During the winter evenings the wife and maid would be spinning in the light of a rush candle and a servant or two carding wool in front of the fire, the husband would be reciting stories and tales, and everyone was happy.'
John Hughes, Llangollen. MS. W.F.M. 3021.
Reference to Weniar, Llansanffraid Glynceiriog.
c. 1800. (Translated from the Welsh)

◆

Is buaine port ná glór na n-éan,
Is buaine focal ná toice an tsaoil.
Irish proverb: A tune is more precious than the song of birds, and a tale more precious than the wealth of the world.'

Foreword to the Third Edition (1995)

Robin Gwyndaf, of the Museum of Welsh Life, has been surveying Welsh folk narrative traditions for more than two decades; in that time, he has interviewed over 2,500 informants, 400 or so of them on tape. This oral testimony – some 600 hours of recordings and 18,000 items of narrative – together with extensive written manuscript material, books and journals – is proof of the exceptionally varied and rich folk narrative tradition of Wales. This book gives the reader a vivid glimpse of that long and creative tradition. The fact that it is again being reprinted shows how well it serves that purpose.

The water-colour map of Wales reproduced on the cover (and available as a poster) was specially commissioned from Margaret D. Jones (of Capel Bangor, Ceredigion), well-known for her paintings of the Mabinogion tales. We are extremely grateful to Mrs Jones, whose map, prepared in collaboration with the author, illustrates the folk tales and traditions associated with 63 districts.

The main part of the book describes these legends and traditions, placing them in their historical and social context. The introduction considers the nature of Welsh folk narrative, and refers to the themes, function, meaning and value of the tales themselves. The final section briefly describes the Welsh folk customs illustrated on the map's borders.

The text is bilingual, and includes a brief glossary and notes on the pronunciation of Welsh names and place-names. We hope that this will make it of interest not only to Welsh and non-Welsh readers, but to those who are learning the language.

Folk tales from very early times have had a very special appeal to people of all ages, creeds and colours; we believe this collection has already shown that it has a similar appeal – in homes and schools, in libraries and other institutions. It also contributes to the Museum's mission

'… to promote a wider knowledge and better understanding of Wales, its history, culture and place in the world …'

Above all, we very much hope that it gives pleasure to its readers.

Colin Ford
Director National Museum of Wales
November 1995

Acknowledgements

Firstly it is my duty to thank the numerous informants all over Wales whom I have had the privilege to interview, or record on tape, during 1964–87. They were always very generous in their welcome and their readiness to share their knowledge.

I also wish to thank sincerely Dr David Dykes, Director of the National Museum of Wales, Dr J. Geraint Jenkins, Curator of the Welsh Folk Museum, and Mr Vincent H. Phillips, Keeper of the Department of Cultural Life, for their full support in the preparation of this volume and the water-colour map of Wales; Mr Hywel G. Rees, Head of Publications and Publicity, for his kind co-operation and great care in producing the poster and book; Mr Eric Broadbent and his colleagues for the photographic work; Mr Paul Rees for his assistance when preparing the poster for exhibition; Mr O. Tudur Jones for preparing the map showing the location of the tales; and Mr Tim Collier for preparing the photographs published in the introduction.

I received valuable assistance from my colleagues: Dr Anne E. Williams, Mrs Sioned Thomas and Dr William Linnard and I am grateful to them. Also to Mr Trefor M. Owen for the extensive use made of his volume *Welsh Folk Customs* in the section on folk customs, and to the University of Wales Press for permission to use *A Gazetteer of Welsh Place-Names*, edited by Elwyn Davies, in the sections relating to the pronunciations and meaning of Welsh words and place-names.

I am particularly indebted to two persons: Mrs Meryl Roberts who typed the book with exceptional care, and Mr Howard Williams who read the book in manuscript and proof form and made numerous valuable suggestions. I greatly appreciate their kind assistance.

Finally, I wish to record my sincere gratitude to Margaret D. Jones for preparing the water-colour map of Wales portraying Welsh legends and traditions with such care and enthusiasm. It was, indeed, a great pleasure for me to collaborate with her.

Robin Gwyndaf

1989

Preface to the second edition

I wish to take this opportunity of expressing my sincere appreciation for the very warm welcome given by readers and reviewers alike to the first edition of *Chwedlau Gwerin Cymru Welsh Folk Tales* and the illustrated map of Wales. I am particularly pleased that the book has been widely used in Welsh schools as part of the national curriculum and by students in Welsh colleges. It has also sold well abroad, and there are plans for the volume, or parts of it, to be translated into French, Russian, Estonian and Japanese.

Reference has already been made in the Bibliography to one cassette, entitled *Storïau Gwerin Cymru* ('Welsh folk narratives'). Since the publication of the first edition of this volume three other cassettes in the Welsh Folk Museum Cassette Series have appeared, all containing material of interest to readers, namely *Blas ar Fyw: Atgofion Serah Trenholme, Nefyn* (reminiscences of Serah Trenholme); *Hiwmor y Chwarelwr* ('the quarryman's humour'), Emrys Evans; and *Brigyn Ir: Sgwrs a Stori yng Nghwmni Siân Williams* ('tales and stories in the company of Siân Williams').

Robin Gwyndaf
1992

Preface to the 5th New Edition by Y Lolfa, 2024

During the first twenty or more years at Amgueddfa Werin Cymru: Welsh Folk Museum, in Sain Ffagan, it was my very good fortune to undertake a survey of the Welsh folk narrative tradition. In 1987 I shared with museum colleagues my desire to publish a beautiful book and poster map of Wales introducing and portraying a selection of Welsh folk legends and tales. It was my great fortune also that I was able to advise the National Museum of Wales to commission the renowned artist Margaret D. Jones, Aberystwyth (but who lived then in Capel Bangor), to paint the map.

In 1988, good news: Margaret Jones accepted the commission to prepare a large water-colour map of Wales portraying the legends and traditions associated with 63 locations. Furthermore, it was my great joy and privilege to work closely with the artist in illustrating each individual painting. The end result was an exceptionally beautiful map of Wales, a truly magnificent work of art. From this map a poster-size print was produced, and each individual painting reproduced to form part of the text in the accompanying book.

Words cannot adequately convey our deep sense of gratitude to Margaret Jones. On behalf of all readers, therefore, I thank her most sincerely now for the immense pleasure her numerous paintings of our Welsh folk tales, including the Mabinogion, have given to so many of us over a long period of time: pleasure – and inspiration. We wish her every blessing.

I also would like to take this opportunity to express my gratitude for all the very warm welcome given to each edition of the book, together with the poster-map. In addition to the kind reception in Wales, the book and map have by now travelled to many parts of the world. Quotations from the book have appeared in a number of languages, including Japanese. Also the French author, Sylvie Ferdinand, has included a version of the book in her publication:

Au Royaume du Dragon rouge. Contes et Légendes du Pays de Galles (Terre de Brume Éditions, Rennes, 2001; pp.273).

Furthermore, it is my pleasure and duty to thank Amgueddfa Cymru – National Museum Wales, for agreeing with my wishes to publish the volume: *Chwedlau Gwerin Cymru: Welsh Folk Tales*, and the map, back in 1989. Also, needless to say, for giving permission now to Y Lolfa to have the book and map reprinted.

It gives me great satisfaction to see the book and map back in print once more. Our folk legends and traditions were never intended to be kept out of sight within the covers of books which are not readily available to the public, or merely to be safely stored in archives, however important that might be. Rather, we safeguard a treasure in order to share it gladly and openly with others, and to provide everyone, whatever their age, colour or creed, with a golden opportunity to appreciate that treasure anew.

Readers will join with me, therefore, in expressing my most sincere thanks to Y Lolfa Press for publishing this new edition. As always, I received from the staff the kindest co-operation. *Canmil diolch*: a 'hundred thousand thanks', and particularly to Lefi Gruffudd.

The Press must also be warmly congratulated for the design of the book. Readers, I am sure, will gratefully appreciate to have in this revised 5th edition all the illustrations in colour. For this I must especially thank Richard Huw Pritchard, one of Y Lolfa's talented designers. Each image in the book was carefully copied from the illustration painted on the map and printed on the poster.

For this 5th edition, the traditional names for the counties of Wales have been used, rather than the new ones introduced at the time the book was first published in 1989. I do, however, use 'Ceredigion' for Cardiganshire.

In addition to persons already mentioned in this preface, it is my great pleasure once again to thank my very good friends, Howard Williams, Clynnog Fawr, and Hywel Williams, Llandaf, Cardiff. As always, they were more than ready with their valuable assistance. Similarly, I cannot begin to thank my own family for their great kindness and constant support: Eleri, my wife, who sadly died, 12 November 2023, and Llyr and Nia, our children.

* * * * *

In this book some guidance has been given concerning the pronunciation of the Welsh language. Also included is a section listing some of the Welsh words most often used in the book, and their meaning. Similarly, the meaning of certain Welsh place-names.

All this is part and parcel of the purpose of publishing the book. One important function, of course, is to entertain. To entertain – but equally as important, to educate.

The need to present the history of Wales in an interesting and meaningful manner to all the inhabitants of our country and beyond, whatever their age or language, has never been more crucial. My hope is that this volume, in Welsh and in English, will be a small contribution towards fulfilling a dream. And this is my dream: that all the people of Wales, and Welsh people living abroad – and, yes, the inhabitants of Britain also – will soon come to appreciate the wealth of our inheritance as a nation, this fair inheritance which constitutes our native language, our literature and our culture. An intrinsic part of that vibrant, wide-ranging culture, is our folk tales and folk traditions, the subject of this present book.

When this book was first published (1989), Amgueddfa Werin Cymru, the Welsh name for the open-air museum at St Fagans, was referred to in English as Welsh Folk Museum (and had been since opening to the public in 1948). In 1995 the English name was changed to Museum of Welsh Life. In 2005 the name was changed yet again to St Fagans National History Museum. But since 2017 the official name is: St Fagans National Museum of History.

Robin Gwyndaf
January, 2024

Cyflwynir y gyfrol hon i gofio yn annwyl iawn am

Eleri Gwyndaf
1937 – 2023

Gyda chanmil diolch am ei chymorth amhrisiadwy
ym maes diwylliant gwerin Cymru.

———

This book is dedicated in memory of my beloved

Eleri

With a thousand thanks for her support and inspiration
in the field of Welsh folk culture.

(Robin Gwyndaf: 31.1.2024).

Introduction

The Welsh Folk Narrative Tradition

> *A grey old man from his corner said:*
> *'From my father I heard a tale;*
> *He heard it from his grandfather,*
> *And after him I, too, remembered it.'*

This verse, translated from a Welsh ballad 'The Old Man of the Woods', by Ellis Roberts, clearly conveys the specific oral nature of the Welsh folk narrative tradition. The term 'folk narrative' is here used to refer to the traditional prose tales, legends, myths, memorates (personal paranormal experiences), jokes and anecdotes which have formed part of the cultural inheritance of the Welsh people from very early times to the present day. The narratives are traditional in the sense that most of them have a long history and were transmitted mainly, though not exclusively, by oral means, in the words of one early chronicler: *iocunde et memoriter* 'with joy and from memory'.

It is not surprising, however, that collectors and writers from the Middle Ages to the present day have recorded and reflected the folk narrative tradition extensively in manuscripts, books, journals, newspaper columns and, more recently, tapes, video cassettes and films. Both the oral and written folk narrative material testify to a long and rich tradition of storytelling in Wales. As early as the ninth century the traditions which Nennius(?) author of *Historia Brittonum* relates about King Arthur, Gwrtheyrn (Vortigern), Taliesin and Garmon, and about wells, lakes and stones are a mirror to a collection of lost tales.

In one scene in the Fourth Branch of the Mabinogi (composed probably during the second half of the eleventh century) Gwydion and his company enter Pryderi's court in Dyfed in the guise of bards:

> 'Lord', said Gwydion, 'it is a custom with us that the first night after one comes to a great man, the chief bard shall have the say. I will tell a tale gladly.' And he, Gwydion, was the best storyteller in the world.

The eleven classic tales known as 'The Mabinogion', described by Professors Gwyn and Thomas Jones as being among 'the finest flowerings of the Celtic genius and, taken together, a masterpiece of our medieval European literature', clearly demonstrate that Wales in medieval times was no exception to other European countries in its folk narrative activity: The Mabinogion have been a source of inspiration to writers, artists and storytellers ever since, and it is fitting that the first item in this book and accompanying poster-map (Afon Alaw) relates to one of the best-known and loved of all the Mabinogion tales, namely the story of Branwen.

No one, probably, has captured the atmosphere of entertainment in early Wales better than Morys Clynnog at the beginning of Gruffydd Robert's Welsh Grammar. Both Morys Clynnog and Gruffydd Robert were Catholic exiles, and publication of this Grammar was begun in Milan in 1567. In its prologue we find the two men one warm afternoon in a pleasant orchard and, being far away from their native country, they converse in Welsh about the days gone by.

> Although the place where we are now is very beautiful, although it is pleasant to see the green leaves offering shelter from the sun, and although it is wonderful to feel this northern breeze blowing beneath the vines to give us joy in this unreasonable heat, which is heavy on everyone who was born and bred in a country as cold as the land of Wales is, yet I have a longing for many things which were to be had in Wales to pass the time away pleasantly and happily while sheltering from the sun on long summer days. Because there,

however warm the weather, there would be comfort and joy to every sort of man. If one wished entertainment, one would have a musician with his harp to play sweet tunes and a melodious singer to sing harp verses according to his desire, whether praise of virtue or satire of evil. It you wish to hear of the custom of the country during our grandfather's time you would find grey old men who could relate to you by word of mouth every remarkable and famous deed which happened throughout the land of Wales a long time ago.

The harp, mentioned by Morys Clynnog, is one of the three traditional musical instruments in Wales. It is referred to in item 9 (Borth-y-gest): 'Dafydd y Garreg Wen', harpist, and in item 21 (Llyn Tegid, Bala Lake): 'Charles y Telynor'. Another traditional instrument was the pipe (hornpipe and bagpipe), mentioned in item 8 (Castellmarch). One of Maelgwn Gwynedd's pipe-players cut a reed to make a new pipe to play before March ap Meirchion, the king with horse's ears. The third traditional instrument was the *crwth*, a six-stringed instrument played with a bow. It is oblong in shape with a flat back, sides and sound-board. It is illustrated on the right hand side of the poster-map.

During the Middle Ages we have very little evidence to show how the ordinary people entertained themselves. From the seventeenth century onwards, however, more information is available. We can now leave the medieval hall of the noble lord with his abundance of wine and food and pleasant company, and can follow the peasant to his cottage or the yeoman to his farmhouse, where on most winter evenings the family and a few neighbours would be gathered around the fire and where one would hear a song, a tale or riddle. We can accompany the farm servants to a *noswaith wau* (knitting evening), partake of the joy of the food and merriment, and shiver with fear while listening to ghost stories. We can also join the inhabitants of a certain parish – men, women and children – and follow them to the village green, a meadow or a mountain pasture (*twmpath chwarae*), on summer evenings, Sundays and the day of the *gwylfabsant* (patron saint's festival).

The Puritan movement of the seventeenth century and the religious revivals of the eighteenth and nineteenth centuries were one of the main reasons for the gradual disappearance of the *gwylfabsant* and other open-air communal gatherings and also of many ancient folk customs and ceremonies. It should be noted, however, that they did not suppress the practice of storytelling. It continued with surprising vigour. Legends relating, for example, to ghosts, Fairies and the Devil, were still being recited, but we notice a distinct process of functional adaptation. The emphasis became even more moralistic and didactic.

Transmission and Communication

Folktales do not exist in a vacuum. They are nurtured in a living community where people communicate with each other daily. They are coloured by language, events, customs and beliefs. Their nature – indeed their very existence – depends on their social context. It is important, therefore, to bear in mind some of the most common occasions when members of the community met for storytelling – occasions we would refer to as the main channels for transmitting the folk narrative tradition from one person to the other.

i.   The family circle – in the company of close neighbours on the hearth. (The most important channel.)

ii. The company of well-known characters and storytellers in towns and villages.

iii. The every-day company of fellow-workers. For example, agricultural workers, coalminers, quarrymen and fishermen.

iv. Workshops and craft centres. For example, the smithy, the flour and woollen mill, the carpenter's and cobbler's workshop.

v.   Occasions of social co-operation between farmers. For example, sheep-shearing day, hay and corn harvest, threshing day, and pig-killing day.

vi. Occasional communal gatherings, pastimes and recreation and the celebration of folk customs and festivities. For example, *yr wylfabsant, noson lawen* (merry evening), *noswaith wau, noson wneud cyflaith* (toffee-making evening), May and Winter's Eve.

vii. The company of fellow-travellers, for example, the drovers.

viii. Fairs and markets.

ix. Inn and taverns.

At this point attention should be drawn also to four general factors that further help us to understand the nature of the Welsh folk narrative tradition and, in particular, its vitality and continuity.

First, the human need which had created the numerous channels of transmission. Most communities were, to a very great extent, self-supporting, and they had to create not only their own work, but also their own culture and entertainment.

Secondly, the favourable conditions that were responsible for maintaining channels of transmission. Generally speaking, Wales was a nation of small, closely-knit communities, in which there was constant reciprocity between individuals, affecting the swiftness with which any new story or anecdote spread like a rumour from person to person. We should also mention the leisurely atmosphere of most kinds of work.

Thirdly, storytelling was only one aspect of entertainment. It was an organic phenomenon – an integral part of a more general activity which included local gossip; reciting and singing of *penillion telyn* (harp stanzas), incidental verse, ballads and folk songs; reciting of riddles and tongue-twisters; games and recreation; customs and festivities.

Fourthly, the informal and unconscious nature of storytelling occasions. Members of the Welsh community rarely met specifically to tell stories. Wherever and whenever two or more people met in happy, relaxed circumstances, storytelling would be a natural and spontaneous outcome of such meetings. Stories were recited during worktime as well as during leisure hours. This point is made by the poet John Davies, 'Taliesin Hiraethog', in a Welsh essay entitled 'Hen

Draddodiadau' ('Old Traditions') in which he refers to the period around the middle of the nineteenth century. This is a translation of the opening paragraph. (MS. private source)

Cerrigydrudion is the highest and most remote parish in Denbighshire. Its coarse-grass hills and heathery mountain pastures are full of interest to the antiquarian. Every mound and hillock, every brook and river are full of old traditions of days gone by, and its rural inhabitants on long winter nights have much delight in reciting the tales and folklore that belong to this land. When the writer was a young boy, shepherding his father's sheep along the banks of the river Alwen and Llyn Dau Ychen ('the lake of the two oxen'), he and his fellow shepherds spent many a happy hour reciting these tales while sitting on a small heap of rushes to keep the sheep from wandering on early summer days.

Continuity and Adaptation

Wales, at least since the Middle Ages, has not seen professional storytellers with a large repertoire of long, heroic wonder tales. However, throughout the later centuries the role of the ordinary storyteller in the Welsh community was an important one. He was the active tradition-bearer who kept the old and the new tales alive by retelling them to others. He always had a ready audience. These were the days when the community not only had to create its own culture and entertainment, but also when the magic of folklore delighted and sustained the spirit of man. In studying Welsh folk narratives, therefore, we notice a remarkable continuity of tradition from very early times to the present day. The reason for this continuity is that the tradition was, and to a great extent still is, a living tradition. From time to time the function of the narratives may have altered, but the actual content of many of them remained almost unchanged. No living folk narrative tradition is static. It develops as the mind of man develops; it changes as the nature of society changes. This explains why so many of the Welsh legends survived the eighteenth and nineteenth-century religious revivals.

What is the situation today? Needless to say, there has been a change. There is certainly less leisure and more haste. Much of our entertainment is ready-made. We have witnessed a gradual breakdown of communal life and traditional channels of transmission. And in many rural areas depopulation and the disappearance of old deeply rooted families with strong kinship connections has gradually affected the continuity of the narrative tradition. Yet, when all is said, the storyteller in Wales today still plays a very important role. If during the twentieth century there has been a weakening and, indeed, disappearance of certain traditional channels of transmission, there are other more contemporary channels or storytelling occasions; the radio and television; the telephone; the student college hostel; the hair dressing salon; the motor car garage; the doctor's surgery; the football and rugby club; the bingo hall and other recreational centres; websites and the social media.

There has been in Wales, as in so many other countries during the twentieth century, a gradual decline in magic. Thus we notice much less emphasis on memorates and local legends illustrating man's belief in the supernatural. By now these narratives seem somehow to be out of touch with the everyday life of the people. In general it could be said that those who recite memorates and legends relating to place names and to historical and pseudo-historical characters and events – these men and women have by now become passive or occasional tradition-bearers. Even so, they still remember many narratives and, as Gwydion remarked in the Fourth Branch of the Mabinogi, they, too, will 'tell a tale gladly' when asked, and especially to whoever is prepared to listen with sympathy and understanding. Although most of these passive or occasional narrators may not themselves believe in the paranormal elements inherent in tales and legends of magic, they will recite them with sincerity and reverence. Their attitude is that of the Carmarthenshire man who confessed:

> *I cannot tell how the truth may be,*
> *I tell the tale as 'twas said to me.*

While these passive storytellers are decreasing, there is certainly no shortage of active storytellers in Wales with a large repertoire of jokes and anecdotes. With the decline in magic and the gradual and general disappearance of legends relating to the supernatural (and it is important to emphasize the word general because belief in ghosts, for example, is still strong), the majority of people in the age of mass media are most interested in true, histrionic narratives: chronicates, anecdotes, gossip and rumour, relating to people's every-day life. Many of these narratives are actually true, of course. For example, chronicates and anecdotes relating to local events and incidents and to local characters. Many other narratives are not. But the important point to remember is that such narratives are often told as if they were true.

In order to give a story an air of reality there is often a tendency for localization – a tale will be linked with a certain locality (although this is not a new phenomenon in folk literature).

This particular family go on their holiday and they take the grandmother with them. She dies, and they place her body on the car roof. On their way home the body disappears.

This so-called urban legend may well have originated in America, but by now the poor old grandmother has travelled to many countries, including Wales! The narrative is always linked with a certain district and a certain person, although the person, usually, is not specifically named. He is 'a friend', or 'a friend of a friend', 'an acquaintance', or 'an acquaintance of an acquaintance'. That is, the narrative is told as if it was true. It is told as an account, a true story – a legend – not as a joke, and it has often been reported in newspapers.

This attempt to give stories an air of truth complies with Linda Dégh's observation on Hungarian communities:

The typical peasant farmer, in his rise towards the bourgeoisie, wants to hear 'true',

i.e. historical stories, reads newspapers, and refuses to listen to tales of wonders which he will stamp out as so many lies.
(*Folktales and Society*, pp. 122, 181.)

But here we seem to have a paradox. Although there would initially be a strong element of truth in many of the narratives – chronicates and anecdotes in particular – as a narrative passes from mouth to mouth it is coloured more and more by man's natural imagination, his instinct for creativity, and his constant need (however strongly he may deny it) to wonder at the marvels of everyday life. Thus what may begin as a simple account of a witty remark or a humorous, untoward incident, may develop eventually into a colourful saga, where the boundary between fact and fantasy becomes very vague indeed. This is particularly true, for example, of white-lie tales. If a tale is told about a character from outside the locality, it is usually easily recognised as a white-lie, but if such a tale is told about a noted witty local character, what seems to be a lie to one listener may be but an extension of the truth to another. It is all part of the wonder and joy of life, where marvels do not necessarily have to happen in faraway lands full of people in possession of a magic wand.

Current Welsh tales display a remarkable combination of old and new themes: ageless topics such as the great passions of life – man's sorrow and joy – and more contemporary subjects which vividly remind us of the modern technological age we live in: drugs, Aids, sports, cremation, computers – even a time machine used by politicians. This story was told by J. W. Goddard, Cerrigydrudion, Clwyd, my brother-in-law:

There was this huge machine which could foretell the state of the Major Powers in five hundred years. First of all Mr Reagan came and entered this machine. To his horror, he saw that all America had completely adopted Communism. Then Mr Gorbachev, the Russian leader, came and what he saw was the complete opposite. All Russia had adopted capitalism. And then, finally, Mrs Thatcher came and stepped briskly inside in all her glory and gazed long at her England. But she soon came out, most upset. 'Oh! Dear me' she said, 'I couldn't understand a single word the people were speaking, they were all talking in Welsh.'

Often many older tales are adapted to reflect new technology, a changing social climate or, indeed, occasionally to express a certain degree of patriotism and pride in one of Wales's national institutions and sports – rugby in particular. Tales of heaven and hell, for example, fit into this category.

This former famous Welsh rugby player dies and enters the golden gates of heaven. He was very worried because he had been a rather dirty player. But the Angel lets him in. 'Oh! Thank you, Saint Peter', the Welshman remarks. 'Saint Peter?' replies the Angel, 'he's on holiday, I'm on duty today.' 'Well, who are you?' And the Angel answers: 'Saint David.'

One obvious characteristic of contemporary Welsh folk narratives is that they are usually quite brief. In fact, some narratives are little more than extended statements or remarks and they remind us of proverbs and proverbial sayings. In the hurly-burly of the motor-car and jet age we have little time for the long story, so we make it short and to the point. This is particularly true of radio and television entertainers and of the comperes of concerts and *nosweithiau llawen*. It is also true in the case of children. The most popular jokes among the young today (and the not-so-young) are riddle-jokes in the form of a brief remark and reply.

'Doctor! Doctor! I feel like a curtain.' Doctor replies: 'Pull yourself together!'

It so happens, however, that a gifted storyteller in a leisurely, happy atmosphere and circumstances will often combine these brief jokes, anecdotes and riddles and develop them into one long, vivid saga.

Another obvious characteristic of contemporary storytelling in Wales is its informality. If storytelling had been an informal and unconscious activity up to the nineteenth century, it became even more so during the twentieth. By today storytelling has become an organic part of the joy of everyday conversation, and it supplies man's everlasting need for a good laugh and to escape, however briefly, from the routine and monotony of life. It is as if the Welsh folktale has completed a full cycle. From the ordinary, every-day speech of the people, the imagination and skill of a gifted narrator and the communal need for entertainment and escapism to the world of wonder, it developed in the Middle Ages into the *märchen* and *novella* tales of magic and romance. By today, the emphasis is on the simpler joke, chronicate and anecdote, which once again closely resembles the everyday speech of the people.

Tale Types and Classification

Folk tales, any more than other aspects of folklore, were never intended to be divided into neatly labelled categories. For the purpose of clarity, however, the tales may very roughly be classified into the following four main groups or streams, but the reader should bear in mind that they often overlap. There are also narratives which are outside the four main groups. There are, for example, a number of animal tales, or fables, with a strong didactic element, similar to Aesop's Fables, tales of romance (*novelle*), and a few very interesting formula tales, such as the various versions of the 'story without an end' (a king offers his daughter in marriage to whosoever can recite a story that lasts for ever), or accumulative tales, on the same pattern as such songs as 'The Twelve Days of Christmas'.

1 Tales of magic

Civilisations may disappear, man's beliefs may change, but his innermost desires remain the same through the ages. And one of his most constant desires was to avoid the routine and certainty of this world and escape into the enchanting world of the unknown. Man in Wales was no exception. The earlier term for magic in Welsh is *hud*, a word of Celtic origin, and the use of this word in the Third Branch of the Mabinogi clearly conveys the atmosphere of the early Welsh tales: *Y mae yma ryw ystyr hud* ('There is here some enchanted meaning'). They are based in a world of wonder where the most ordinary youth has the power of a magician and where fields and trees disappear at the wink of an eye.

By today few tales of magic (*märchen*) still exist in current Welsh oral tradition, and these are usually considerably shortened versions. Even so, they give us a brief glimpse of the ever-present atmosphere of enchantment which was so characteristic of the medieval world: the tale of the birds of Llyn Syfaddan (Llan-gors Lake, item 43); the tale of the magic ring which gives to a poor boy anything he wishes; the tale of the magic mill which still grinds salt at the bottom of the Welsh sea; and the tale of the monk of Maes-glas (Greenfield, Flintshire), who listened to a nightingale's song, and when he returned to his monastery found it in ruins and all his colleagues dead many years since. In many of these tales we have the same motif of the supernatural passage of time as we find in our fairy legends; in the legend of King Arthur on the Isle of Afallon; and in the tale of Branwen, where the Birds of Rhiannon sing a most beautiful song for seven years to the seven men at Harlech.

2 Belief in the supernatural

If there is by now a shortage in Wales of long international wonder tales (*märchen*), there is no shortage of brief local legends (*sagen*) illustrating man's belief in the supernatural. These belief legends refer, for example, to the Fairies; mine Knockers; the Devil; witches; magicians and wise men; ghosts; apparitions, such as death omens; giants; mythological animals, such as dragons, winged serpents, black dogs and water monsters, like the *afanc* (item 38); and supernatural events and incidents, such as the remarkable wheat which grew on the farm of Henry Williams, Llanllwchaearn (29) and the mysterious Egryn Chapel lights seen during the 1904–5 Revival (25).

Because these legends are based on various folk beliefs, it is important to remember that the content of many of them was once, at least, believed to be true (and this, of course, is one of the main differences between a folk legend and a folk tale or story). When a person actually experiences a certain belief we may refer to this experience as a 'memorate'. It describes a supra-normal or paranormal experience undergone by the narrator or by an acquaintance or ancestor. Memorates relate mainly to personal narratives and to what we could term the individual or family tradition. With the passage of time many of these empirical narratives have become stereotyped, and the content is more schematic and impersonal. They follow a certain plot formula which can travel easily from one district to another. They correspond to the *sagen* in form and style and are well on the way to developing into local belief legends and becoming part of the collective tradition of the community.

In the course of time more and more motifs relating to the world of fantasy and the fabulous are added to the 'true' legend. Often they are told as stories, and although the local element is still very obvious, the terms 'migratory legends' and 'fabulates' used by scholars to refer to such narratives aptly conveys their nature. Many of the legends relating to the Fairies, the Devil and ghosts, and described in this book, belong to this category.

3 History and tradition

Medieval storytellers and poets in many countries were expected to be well versed in the history, traditions and genealogy of their people; for example, the Teutonic *scop*, the Hindu *sūta*, the Irish *fili*, the *bardos* of the Continental Celts, and the Welsh *pencerdd*. In many countries the same is true also of the post-medieval storytellers and poets. It is true, for example, of the Irish *seanchaí* and the Welsh storyteller.

In the *Trioedd Cerdd* ('the poetic or song triads') as recorded in the Red Book of Hergest's version of the grammar attributed to Einion Offeiriad are the following words: 'Three things that give amplitude to a poet: knowledge of histories (*ystoriau*), the poetic art, and old verse.' *Ystoriau* (stories) in this context, to quote Rachel Bromwich, refers to the 'national inheritance of ancient traditions'. (*Trioedd Ynys Prydein. The Welsh Triads*, p.lxxi). The word is a late borrowing from the Latin *historia*, and the repertoire of a number of cultured tradition-bearers in Wales today – men who often combine the two roles of local historian and poet – is a remarkable reminder of the medieval triad. To give a brief glimpse of the wealth of material included in this 'national inheritance of ancient traditions', a cross-section of which is mentioned in this present book, we could refer to the following main categories of legends and traditions relating to:

i.   Early historical and pseudo-historical persons such as King Arthur (items 12, 53, 55); Myrddin (Merlin, 51); Taliesin (27, 34); and the Welsh Saints (3, 13, 16, 45, 47, 50, 62).

ii.   Famous and remarkable Welshmen, such as Llywelyn, the Last Prince of Wales (42) and Owain Glyndŵr (19, 24), national heroes; Barti Ddu, sea pirate (48); Twm Siôn Cati, folk hero (37).

iii. Local and historical events, such as the adventures of Gwylliaid Cochion Mawddwy ('The Red Bandits of Mawddwy') during the sixteenth century (23) and the landing of the French at Fishguard in 1797 (46).

iv.   Place-names and physical features such as fields, stones, caves, wells, lakes, rivers and bridges. Many of the narratives in this last category are onomastic. They explain the origin of a name or the location of a physical feature. For example, Devil's Bridge (32) and Beddgelert (10) – a name connected with the international legend of 'the man who killed his dog'.

One recurring element in these legends is the close interrelationship which exists between history and tradition, fact and fiction. The description of an eighteenth-century murder may be a fact, but is the irremovable blood-stain on the wall merely a folk belief?

4 Humour

There has been in Wales, as in so many other countries, a long and diverse tradition of reciting humorous tales which have a very special appeal to all members of the community. These tales can be subdivided roughly into the following five main groups.

i. Humorous stories and jokes generally known throughout Wales, often with similar versions in other countries and most of the characters being stereotyped.

ii. Humorous stories and anecdotes based mainly upon humour of speech (wit), which reflect the interest, work and personality of a certain social group, such as the coalminers of South Wales or the quarrymen of North Wales.

iii. Humorous jokes and anecdotes relating to actual well-known local characters. Many of these narratives form cycles – the same story being told about different characters in different areas. A good example is those most interesting characters in the villages and towns of Wales up to the beginning of the twentieth century who had a never-ending repertoire of white-lie tales and who, before the days of radio and television, were non-paid first-class entertainers with a command of colourful, idiomatic language, a natural gift for storytelling, and a remarkable imagination.

iv. Humorous anecdotes relating to local characters, but whose narratives are not so well known outside their own locality.

v. Humorous anecdotes relating to untoward local incidents, referred to in Welsh as *troeon trwstan*

Selection of Tales

In deciding on the choice of tales to be illustrated and described there were three main considerations. Firstly, every attempt was made to select tales and traditions which are fairly well known and have long been regarded as an important aspect in the folk inheritance of the Welsh people. Secondly, to select items which reflect, as far as is possible, the very wide spectrum of the Welsh folk narrative tradition. Thirdly, to acquire a fairly balanced geographical representation. Needless to say, the final choice and total number of tales included depended on the number of illustrations that could be fitted onto the accompanying map.

Only tales whose location could be established with reasonable accuracy are included. This is the main reason why the majority of items are not tales or stories, as such, but local legends and traditions which are inseparably linked with various districts. The majority of the legends relate to mythological beings, such as the Fairies, the Devil, ghosts, giants, dragons and water monsters; famous and remarkable heroes and characters from Welsh history; and to place-names, lakes, well, caves, stones and bridges.

The characters in tales of humour are often stereotyped, and the narratives, as such, are not always localized. It was not possible, therefore, to give due representation to the rich tradition of humorous tales, with a few exceptions, such as the anecdotes associated with Twm Siôn Cati (37).

One obvious omission are items relating to the colourful characters who recited white-lie tales, for example, Shemi Wâd (James Wade), Goodwick, near Fishguard, and the equally picturesque characters well known for their wit and humour, for example, Twm Weunbwll (Thomas Phillips), Glandŵr, Pembrokeshire. These two characters could easily have been included but for the existence of other important traditions close by associated with the landing of the French at Fishguard (46) and the Rebecca Riots at Yr Efail Wen, Pembrokeshire (49).

Themes, Function and Meaning

The prime function of the tales presented in this book was to entertain. At times certain tales (relating, for example, to the world of magic and the supernatural) helped man to escape, if even for a short while, from life's routine and worries. But they represented much more than escapism through entertainment. As already noted, many of them are folk legends based on folk beliefs and personal experiences. It is tempting for us, in the sophistication of the twentieth century, to regard the legends as merely a reflection of our forefather's superstitions. It is important to remember, however, that to our ancestors these legends had a specific function and meaning and a kernel of truth which was accepted with reverence and sincerity.

The narratives reveal man's deepest feelings: his joy and sorrow, his aspirations and fears. They reveal his reaction to life's wonder and mystery; his attitude towards his fellow men; and, occasionally, his concern with death – especially the dead who return in the form of a spirit or ghost to torment the living.

Many of the legends and traditions are an expression of man's innate fear. He must refrain from tempting fate and incurring the displeasure of the gods. In ancient days he would stroke a tree in the woods to secure the blessing of the forest god, and today people still say 'touch wood' – just in case. The narratives reflect his fear of the unknown, witchcraft, the evil eye, disease and death. He depends on charms. He needs an anchor and security. At times he puts his faith in God, at other times in the wise man, *y dyn hysbys* (item 31).

There are certain things which are forbidden to man, certain taboos which must never be broken. There is one tree in the Garden of Eden whose fruit must not be eaten; there is a well at Cantre'r Gwaelod (the Lowland Hundred) whose cover must be replaced to prevent it from overflowing (34); there is one door at Gwales in the tale of Branwen which must not be opened; there is a treasure under a stone or *cromlech* which is not to be disturbed.

The punishment for disobedience, greed and cruelty is anguish and death. There is a bell in King Arthur's Cave (55) which must not be sounded, but the young man who enters the cave inadvertently touches it in his greedy quest for money and is severely beaten. In one version of the Cantre'r Gwaelod legend, the sixteen fair cities and all their inhabitants are drowned because the drunken Seithennin, the keeper of the floodgates, neglects his duties. Cruel princes are responsible for the drowning of the lands beneath Llyn Tegid (Bala Lake, 21), and Llyn Syfaddan (Llan-gors Lake, 43). Pennard Castle (54) is engulfed by a sand storm because the prince drives away the Fairies dancing on the Castle green, and the inhabitants of Conwy are afflicted by a fish famine because of their cruel treatment of a mermaid (13).

Man's constant battle against evil, therefore, is a major theme in Welsh folk tales. They have a specific didactic and moralistic function: to convince their listeners of the eventual triumph of goodness over evil. The Devil must be defeated or outwitted – as the old woman successfully accomplishes in the Devil's Bridge tale (32); evil spells must be cast away; the witch's curse must be negated; and God's divine power, the miracles and virtue of the saints, and the joy and blessing of man's love and friendship must always be proclaimed.

Welsh folk tales were also an important source of inspiration. Narratives relating to history and tradition remind us that in Wales, as elsewhere, the link between the past and the present was a very real one. Folk memory made people conscious of a long and vivid history. The term *hyd y nawfed ach*, 'until the ninth generation', appears often in Welsh tales (e.g. Llyn Syfaddan, 43). The genealogist and herald-bard enjoyed a prominent role in Welsh society, and today interest in family history is as alive as ever.

In many of the Welsh tales past, present and future are combined. The 'Golden Age' of yesterday is yet to come. The tales relate to heroes of past ages: Arthur, Merlin, Taliesin, Gwenllian, Llywelyn, Owain Glyndŵr. But these were no ordinary men and women who once trod the land of Wales – they did not die, their memory did not fade into oblivion. Their names still live on in the consciousness of people, and their courage and leadership are still a source of inspiration to the Welsh in the twentieth century.

Evaluating the Tradition

If, in conclusion, one was asked what is the value of Welsh folk tales? What do we learn from listening to them? Why should they be safeguarded today and retold yet again to a new audience? The answer would be a threefold one.

Firstly, the narratives merit our attention because of their aesthetic qualities. Many of them are minor works of art, displaying a sincerity of purpose, vividness of characterization, a simplicity of style and form, and a gifted use of language.

Secondly, an understanding of the narratives and their function and the role of the narrator in the community help us to improve our understanding of the whole community.

Thirdly, the more we study these tales and their social context, the closer we come to an understanding of the nature of human culture and, indeed, of life itself. A study of the tales' origin, development and morphology helps us to remember that there have been four main stages in the long history of our country: prehistoric Wales, once part of the joint continents of Europe and Asia; Wales as part of the Celtic countries; Wales as part of the Island of Britain; and Wales as a more or less independent unit. Some of the narratives tell us something about pre-Christian gods and heroes, such as Gwyn ap Nudd (Nantmel, 39). Fairy lake legends (e.g. Llyn y Fan Fach, 44) may suggest a type of primitive lake dwelling (*crannog*). And the *Ychen Bannog* legends (Llanddewibrefi, 38) are reminiscent of the kind of wild cattle which roamed Britain in pre-Roman times.

By studying folk tales we are given a glimpse, as it were, of the marvels of the human brain and the development of man's thought through the centuries. For instance, the numerous onomastic tales which endeavour to explain the meaning of place-names such as Beddgelert (10), reflect man's creative impulse and vivid imagination.

From the Latin word *historia* have derived the Welsh words for both 'histories' (*ystoriau*) and 'meaning' (*ystyr*). It is of significance, too, that the early Welsh word for storyteller was *y cyfarwydd*, lit. 'the familiar one'. His task was *cyfarwyddo* (to direct). It is believed that the

Welsh word *gweled* ('to see'), and the Irish word *fili* (gen. *filed*) both derive from the same Indo-European stem. The Welsh *cyfarwydd*, like the Irish *fili*, was a poet – a visionary, an interpreter, a teacher. He was a leader and inspirer of his people – the one who helped them to 'see'; to visualize the invisible; to give meaning to the meaningless.

Pronunciation of Welsh Words and Place-Names

The following general principles (based on Elwyn Davies, ed., *Rhestr o Enwau Lleoedd: A Gazetteer of Welsh Place-Names*, University of Wales Press, Cardiff, 1957) are intended to assist the English reader in the correct pronunciation of Welsh words and place-names mentioned in this book. 'Welsh', to quote Elwyn Davies, 'is a much more phonetic language than English and the sounds represented by the letters are, on the whole, very consistent … Some of the sounds of the Welsh tongue are, however, as different from those of English as are the sounds of any other foreign language, and they need to be similarly learnt … The only really difficult sound is that represented by the letter *ll*.'

The consonants have each one sound only.

b, **d**, **h**, **l**, **m**, **n**, **p**, **t**, have the same sound as in English.

c, is always hard, as in *cat* and is the equivalent in sound of the English *k*; it is never soft as in *city*, e.g. *caer* = Eng. *k-aye-r*.

ch, is the same harsh, throaty sound as in the Scottish *loch* when properly pronounced, or the German *nach*.

dd, represents a different sound from the English *d*; it has the same sound as *th* in *this*, e.g. *ddu* = Eng. *thee*.

f, has the same sound as the English *v*; e.g. *fan* = Eng. *van*.

ff, is the equivalent of the English *f*; e.g. *ffynnon* = Eng. *fun-on*.

g, is always hard as in *gate*, never soft as in *ginger*, e.g. Gwynedd.

r, is trilled as in *merry*.

s, is hard as in *essay*; it never has the *z* sound as in *nose*.

The following double letters, which are elements in the Welsh alphabet, represent distinctive sounds:

ng, is almost always as in *long*, but very occasionally it has the value of *ng + g* as in *longer*, e.g. *Bangor = Bang-gor*.

ph, has the same sound as in English words like *phone*.

rh, is a trilled *r* followed by the aspirate.

th, is as in *thin*, and is different from the sound in *this* and *breathe*, which is represented by *dd* in Welsh.

The vowels in Welsh are **a**, **e**, **i**, **o**, **u**, **w**, **y**. Unlike the consonants they have two values, short and long.

Long **a** = Eng. *ah*, as in *palm*, e.g. in *glas* the *a* is long, not short as in Eng. *lass*.

Short **a** is a pure, flat sound as in French *à la* and has nothing of the *ae* sound so often given to *a* in English, e.g. in *carn* the vowel sound is open and unlike that in the English equivalent *cairn*.

Long **e** is also given a pure vowel sound rarely heard in southern English but is similar to *a* in *face*, *gate*, in northern pronunciations, e.g. *tre* is similar in sound to the French *très*.

Short **e** is as in *get*.

Long **i** is the *ee* sound in words like *machine*, e.g. *crib = kreeb*.

Short **i** is as in *pin*.

Long **o** is as in *door*, e.g. *dôl* – Eng. *dole*.

Short **o** is as in *not*, e.g. *morfa = morr-vah*.

Short **u**, as pronounced in North Wales, is a sound that is not known in English. It is not unlike the French u but is not rounded. In South Wales the sound approximates to long and short *i* as described above.

Long **w** is the *oo* sound in *pool*, e.g. *drws* = *drooss*.

Short **w** is the *oo* sound in *good*, e.g. *cwm* – Eng. *coomb*.

y, long and short, has two sounds, the 'clear' sound which is similar to the Welsh *i*, and the 'obscure' sound which, when long, is like *u* in *further*, and when short is like *u* in *gun*, e.g. in *mynydd* the first *y* is obscure and the second is clear, thus *mun-eedd*.

In general, vowels are short when followed by two or more consonants or by c, ng, m, p, t, and long when followed by b, ch, d, f, ff, g, s, th.

Stress. As a rule the accent is on the penultimate syllable in Welsh, e.g. Llanddóna, Llanllwcháearn. Where the stress is thrown forward on to the last syllable this is usually indicated by the use of a hyphen, e.g. Borth-y-gést, Aber-sóch. A few place-names are so familiar that it is not considered necessary to indicate the stress by inserting hyphens, e.g. Pontypridd (= Pont-y-pridd), Llanrwst (= Llan-rwst).

Glossary

English translations of Welsh words and place-names in the text are indicated by the use of a lower-case initial, single quotation marks and round brackets, e.g. Cae'r Fendith ('the field of blessing') (item 29). The translation is given for the benefit of non-Welsh readers and should not be regarded as an acceptable alternative to the Welsh name. Where there is a recognised Welsh and English form for a name, initial capitals are used, e.g. Bedd y Lleidr – The Robber's Grave (item 30).

Mutation. Certain initial consonants in Welsh are mutated, for example when elements in place-names are compounds. The following table and general principles (based on Elwyn Davies, *A Gazetteer of Welsh Place-Names*) may assist the non-Welsh reader in tracing the radical forms of mutated consonants.

	Radical	p	t	c	b	d	g	m	ll	rh
	Soft	b	d	g	f	dd	–	f	l	r
Mutation	Nasal	mh	nh	ngh	m	n	ng	no change		
	Spirant	ph	th	ch	no change			no change		

The initial consonant of a feminine singular noun is softened after the definite article, as in Llyn y Fan Fach (Llyn + y + ban + bach).

The initial consonant of the noun is softened after the preposition *ar*, as in Pontarfynach (Pont + ar + mynach); after the preposition *yn* it undergoes a nasal mutation, as in Llanfair-ym-Muallt (Llan + Mair + yn + buallt).

The initial consonant of an adjective undergoes a soft mutation after a feminine singular noun, as in Rhos Goch (Rhos + coch), Yr Efail Wen (Yr + efail + gwen (gwyn)).

The initial consonant of the second element of a compound undergoes a soft mutation, as in Glasgwm (Glas + cwm).

The initial consonant of the genitive is softened after a feminine singular noun, as in Llanfor (Llan + môr); the initial of a personal name in the genitive may be softened after a masculine singular noun, as in Tyddewi (Tŷ + Dewi), Llangollen (Llan + Collen), Llangurig (Llan + Curig), Llanfihangel (Llan + Mihangel).

Many Welsh place-names are composed of the two elements *llan* (church, enclosure, village) + the name of a saint, as in the last three examples above. The word *llan*, however, is not always followed by the name of a saint; e.g. Llan-gors (Llan + cors = bog), Llandaf (Llan + Taf = river).

abaty	abbey		*Calan Gaeaf*	Winter Calend, Winter's Eve
aber	estuary, confluence		*Calan Mai*	May Calend, May Day
afanc	water monster		*calennig*	new year's gift
afon	river		*capel*	chapel
Annwfn	The Underworld		*carn*	cairn
ar	on, upon, over, by		*carnedd*	cairn, tumulus
bach	(adj.) small, little		*carreg*	stone
ban	peak, bare hill, beacon		*castell*	castle
bedwen	birch		*cawr*	giant
bedd	grave		*cefn*	ridge
bryn	hill		*cloch*	bell
cae	field, enclosure		*coch*	red
caer	fort, stronghold		*coed*	trees, wood, forest

cors	bog	*gwaseila*	wassailing
craig	rock	*gwrach*	witch, hag
croes	cross	*gwylfabsant*	patron saint's festival
croesffordd	cross-road	*Gwyliau, Y*	Christmastide
cwm	valley, combe	*gwyn*	white
Cŵn Annwn	Dogs of the Underworld	*Ladi Wen*	'white lady', ghost
cwys	furrow	*llan*	church, enclosure, village
cyfarwydd	storyteller	*llwy serch*	love spoon
chwedl	legend	*llwybr*	path
dawns	dance	*llyn*	lake
Diafol, Y	The Devil	*llys*	court, hall
dinas	hill fortress	*maen*	stone
dôl	meadow	*maes*	field, plain
draig	dragon	*mawr*	great, big
dryw	wren	*moel*	bare hill, bald
du	black	*môr*	sea
dŵr	water	*mynachlog*	monastery
dyffryn	valley	*mynwent*	cemetery
Dyn Hysbys	Wise Man	*mynydd*	mountain
efail	smithy	*Nadolig*	Christmas
eglwys	church	*nant*	brook
ffordd	road, way	*nos*	night, evening
ffynnon	well, spring	*noson lawen*	'merry evening', light entertainment
gaseg fedi, y	harvest mare		
glyn	valley, glen	*noswaith wau*	'knitting evening'
gwaun	moor, mountain pasture	*ogof*	cave

pen	head, top, end	*traddodiad*	tradition
plas	hall, mansion	*tre(f)*	homestead, hamlet, town
pont	bridge	*tŷ*	house
porth	harbour, gateway	*Tylwyth Teg*	Fairies
pwll	pool, pit	*wen*	see gwyn
rhos	moorland	*ychen*	oxen
sant	saint	*Ychen Bannog*	'long horned oxen'
tafarn	tavern, inn	*yn*	in
telyn	harp	*ynys*	island
telynor	harpist	*ysbryd*	ghost, spirit
tir	land		

Welsh Folk Tales: Brief Synopsis

1 **Afon Alaw, Anglesey**
Branwen's Grave

2 **Llanddona, Anglesey**
The Witches of Llanddona

3 **Ynys Llanddwyn, Anglesey**
Dwynwen, the patron saint of Welsh lovers

4 **Clynnog Fawr, Caernarfonshire**
Saint Beuno and the curlew. Beuno's chest and well

5 **Nant Gwrtheyrn, Caernarfonshire**
i Gwrtheyrn, the traitor
ii The romance of Rhys and Meinir

6 **Aberdaron, Caernarfonshire**
Dic Aberdaron, notable character and linguist

7 **Ynys Enlli (Bardsey Island)**
The island of saints

8 **Castellmarch, Caernarfonshire**
March ap Meirchion and his horse's ears

9 **Borth-y-gest, Caernarfonshire**
Dafydd y Garreg Wen: harpist

10 **Beddgelert, Caernarfonshire**
Gelert, Llywelyn the Great's hound

11 **Dinas Emrys, Caernarfonshire**
The Red Dragon

12 **Yr Wyddfa (Snowdon), Caernarfonshire**
i The eagles of Snowdon
ii Arthur and Rhita the giant

13 **Conwy, Caernarfonshire**
i The mermaid and the famine in Conwy
ii Saint Bride and the fish

14 **Ffynnon Eilian, Denbighshire**
The most famous witching well in Wales

15 **Llanefydd, Denbighshire**
Catherine of Berain and her four husbands

16 **Treffynnon (Holywell), Flintshire**
Saint Winifred's Well: the most famous holy well in Wales

17 **Rhuthun, Denbighshire**
Huail's stone. Huail fab Caw beheaded by Arthur

18 **Mynydd Hiraethog, Denbighshire**
A cairn of stones in memory of the young lad who died in the snow

19 **Valle Crucis, Denbighshire**
Owain Glyndŵr and the Abbot of Valle Crucis

20 **Llangar, Merionethshire**
Llangar Church: 'the church of the white stag'

21 **Llyn Tegid (Bala Lake), Merionethshire**
i Tegid Foel and the drowning of the old town of Bala
ii The drowning of Charles the harpist

22 **Pennant Melangell, Montgomeryshire**
Melangell, patron saint of hares

1

Afon Alaw, Anglesey

In the second branch of the Mabinogi (the classical Welsh tales, written sometime during the second half of the eleventh century), we are told how Bendigeidfran led an army to Ireland to avenge the wrong done to his sister Branwen. In the ensuing battle the heroic warriors of the 'Island of the Mighty' were all killed except for seven men. These seven returned to Wales, together with Branwen, and the head of Bendigeidfran, their lord. 'And they came to land at Aber Alaw in Talebolion. And then they sat down and rested. Then she looked on Ireland and the Island of the Mighty, what she might see of them. "Alas, Son of God", said she, "woe is me that ever I was born: two good islands have been laid waste because of me!" And she heaved a great sigh, and with that broke her heart. And a four-sided grave was made for her, and she was buried there on the bank of the Alaw.'

Until the beginning of the nineteenth century there was a mound on the banks of the river Alaw, near Llanddeusant, Anglesey, known locally as Bedd Branwen ('Branwen's grave') and Carn Branwen ('Branwen's cairn'). In 1813, however, local farmers needed stones for building. The mound was destroyed and a stone chest discovered with an urn inside containing human ashes. One large stone still remains where the mound once stood and is known to this day as Bedd Branwen or Carreg Branwen ('Branwen's stone').

2
Llanddona, Anglesey

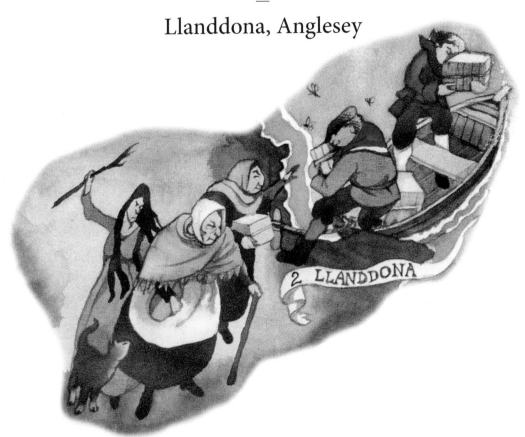

The 'Witches of Llanddona', Anglesey, are certainly among the most famous of Welsh witches. It is said that they were expelled from their native country (Scandinavia, according to tradition) many centuries ago for practising witchcraft, cast adrift in a boat without rudder or oar and left at the mercy of the sea. They eventually landed in Anglesey, and when the native Welsh failed to drive them away they settled on the steep slopes between the village of Llanddona and the sea. Cyrdeddi Bach, Belan Wen, Bwlch y Groes and a few other places in the district are still tenuously connected with them, and even now the names of the witches Bela Fawr ('Big Bella'), Lisi Blac and Siân Bwt ('Little Siân') feature in oral tradition. Siân Bwt was barely four foot tall. She was a dark-faced woman, poorly dressed, with two thumbs on her left hand. The witches came ashore almost dead from hunger and thirst and, according to tradition, commanded that a spring of clear water should appear on the beach. The water issued forth at their feet.

They lived by begging and cursing and it was believed that their power descended from one generation to the next, especially from mother to daughter. They were greatly feared. No one dared refuse them anything or bid against them in the market for fear of being bewitched. If an animal became ill or died, or if, during the close weather in summer, the cream in the butter churn was long in 'breaking', who was to be blamed but the witches? It was also believed that they could transform themselves into hares to avoid being caught while milking the cows. They often met near Ffynnon Oer ('the cold well') to chant their curses, one of which is translated here: 'Let him wander for many centuries; and at each step a style; on each style a fall; in each fall a breaking of bone; neither the largest nor the smallest but the neck bone every time'.

Their husbands lived by smuggling, and it was almost impossible to overcome them. They fought like lions, and when tired would release a fly hidden in their cravats which would assail their opponents' eyes, thus blinding them.

So great was the impact of these foreign exiles that even today people still refer to the inhabitants of this Anglesey community, tongue in cheek, as 'The Witches of Llanddona'.

3 YNYS LLANDDWYN

3

Ynys Llanddwyn, Anglesey

Llanddwyn is a 65 acre island off the coast of Anglesey, near Newborough, and is associated with Dwynwen, the patron saint of Welsh lovers. Dwynwen was one of Brychan Brycheiniog's reputed twenty four daughters and one of the most beautiful. She was deeply in love with Maelon Dafodrill. But Brychan had already arranged for her to marry another prince. In his anger Maelon raped Dwynwen and left her. Saddened with grief, she retreated to a lonely wood and prayed to God to relieve her of her great love for Maelon. When she was asleep an angel gave her a sweet drink which completely cured her. In her dream she saw the same drink being given to Maelon, but he was transformed into a lump of ice. God then gave Dwynwen three wishes. First she wished that Maelon be unfrozen; secondly that God might answer all requests made by her on behalf of true lovers and, thirdly, that she should never again wish to be married. All her wishes were granted. She devoted her life to serve God, and the remains of her church can be seen today on the island.

From the Middle Ages until the eighteenth century many lovers visited Dwynwen's shrine to ask her blessing. They also believed that the course of their love could be foretold by the movements of a rare sacred fish in Dwynwen's Well, a well known today as Ffynnon Fair ('Mary's well'). Saint Dwynwen's Festival was celebrated on the 25th of January. In recent years the custom has been revived, and Welsh Saint Dwynwen greetings cards are published for use by lovers.

4

Clynnog Fawr, Caernarfonshire

The church at Clynnog Fawr, a village on the main road between Caernarfon and Nefyn, is dedicated to Saint Beuno about whom numerous local legends are told. It is said that he received land at Clynnog from Gwyddaint, a cousin of Cadwallon, King of Gwynedd. In order to bless and seal the gift, Beuno carved with his own thumb a cross on a stone known today as Maen Beuno ('Beuno's stone') which is kept at the church. The most well-known legend relates how Saint Beuno one day was crossing the shallow sea from Clynnog to Llanddwyn island when he accidentally dropped his book of sermons into the water. The book was carried away out of his reach by the waves, but a curlew picked it up and placed it safely on a stone. As token of his gratitude Saint Beuno prayed to God that the bird, henceforth, be blessed and safeguarded. His prayer was answered and that is why it is very difficult to find the curlew's nest.

When Saint Beuno died three monasteries, according to tradition, argued for the right to bury his body: Bardsey Island, Beddgelert and Clynnog. But then a miracle occurred. The coffin-bearers stayed overnight at a place not far from Clynnog – called ever since Ynys yr Arch ('coffin island') – and the following morning, to their great surprise, they saw three coffins. Each of the three monasteries were then satisfied, although the monks of Clynnog claimed that they had received the true coffin!

An ancient heavy chest, known as *Cyff Beuno*, which was carved out of a single tree trunk, may still be seen at Clynnog Church. Until the nineteenth century calves bearing Saint Beuno's mark (a natural slit on the ear) were sold and the money placed in the chest as an offering. Saint Beuno's Well is about two hundred yards from the church and was once renowned as a healing well capable of curing epileptic children and people of weak constitution.

5

Nant Gwrtheyrn, Caernarfonshire

Since the early fifties until recently Nant Gwrtheyrn, near Llithfaen, Pwllheli, was a deserted village, enclosed between the sea and steep slopes. The two best-known traditions connected with it are steeped in tragedy which has no doubt pervaded the feelings of many who have looked down on the empty village and sensed that it was fated to die.

The earliest tradition is linked with the fifth-century Gwrtheyrn (Vortigern), portrayed in legend and history as a notorious British king and traitor who betrayed his own people to the Saxons. (See also item 11.) He was forced to leave Dinas Emrys and fled to Nant Gwrtheyrn. Monks had sworn that as punishment for his misdeeds Gwrtheyrn's death would not be a natural one. Some believed that he and his castle were burnt; others believed that he was killed by lightning or that he was forced to jump to his death from a huge rock overlooking the sea, called till this day Carreg y Llam ('leap stone').

A much later and more popular tradition relates the sombre tale of two lovers from the Nant, Rhys and Meinir. On the day of their wedding the young men came to carry the bride to church and Meinir, following an old custom, pretended to escape. She hid in a hollow tree, but she was unable to extract herself and was, for a long time, lost. Rhys became an insane wanderer with only his faithful dog as companion. One day the hollow tree was split open by lightning and the skeleton of his beloved Meinir fell out. Rhys died soon afterwards heart-broken and the two lovers were buried in the same coffin. According to another version of the story Rhys died before Meinir's body was found. Three monks from nearby Clynnog on a Christian mission had experienced opposition from the inhabitants of Nant Gwrtheyrn and, as punishment, had cursed the people and made three prophecies: first, that no two lovers from

Nant Gwrtheyrn would ever marry; secondly, not one of the inhabitants would be buried in consecrated ground; and, thirdly, the village itself would eventually die. The second prophecy was fulfilled, it is said, when the horse pulling the cart carrying Meinir's body to be buried at Clynnog Church failed to climb the steep hill from the Nant. It plunged over the cliff to the sea dragging the cart and coffin with it.

Since the late nineteen seventies, with the foundation there of the Welsh Language Centre, life has once more returned to Nant Gwrtheyrn.

6 ABERDARON

6

Aberdaron, Caernarfonshire

Belonging to Sgubor Bach, a farm near Aberdaron, is a field where the cottage of Cae'r Eos once stood. This was the birth-place of Richard Robert Jones (1780–1843), a notable character known throughout Wales as 'Dic Aberdaron', and the subject of many a tale. His father was a ship carpenter and he employed his son as an apprentice. But it seems that young Dic had very little interest in his father's work and left home at an early age. With a stock of books in his pockets, a cat at his side, a ram's horn around his neck and often wearing a curious hareskin hat, he spent his life travelling the country and learning up to fifteen languages. Although he had received no formal education he began to learn Latin when he was twelve years of age.

It was believed that he also had the gift of summoning demons. At times they appeared in the form of piglets called by Dic 'Cornelius' Cats'. Once, when the reapers at Methlem farm, near Aberdaron, were having difficulty harvesting corn in a field full of thistles Dic called for the assistance of his demonic friends, and the whole field was reaped in a matter of minutes.

He was at St. Asaph, Clwyd, when he died, and it was there that he was buried. A short biography of Dic Aberdaron by H. Humphreys, Caernarfon was published. He is also the subject of a well-known poem by Sir T. H. Parry-Williams which concludes with the following lines:

> 'Let us respect his memory, one and all;
> let us exalt this linguist and cat lover from Llŷn.
>
> If he was obsessed by thumbing through dictionaries and fondling a cat,
> fair play to Dic, not every one is obsessed by the same thing.' (Translation)

7

Ynys Enlli (Bardsey Island)

For centuries Bardsey Island, two miles off the tip of the Llŷn Peninsula, was a sacred destination for pilgrims and saints from Wales and beyond. According to tradition, twenty thousand saints are buried there, and over the years many bones have been discovered by the islanders. Completion of three pilgrimages to Enlli was regarded at one time as being equivalent to one pilgrimage to Rome. Some of the pilgrims' paths are still remembered by the inhabitants of Llŷn. For example, at the old Gegin Fawr ('the big kitchen') in Aberdaron they would linger awhile to eat their last meal on the mainland before crossing the water, and in a rock at the foot of Mynydd Mawr at Uwchmynydd and facing Enlli there is a well called Ffynnon Fair ('Mary's well'). It is said that the pilgrims used to walk down Grisiau Mair ('Mary's steps'), drink water from this well and then recite their last prayers before venturing to cross the strait from Porth Meudwy ('the hermit's port') to Enlli.

By today virtually no one lives on the island throughout the year, but in summer especially it is still a retreat for visitors and naturalists, and the tradition of the 'twenty thousand saints' is still very much alive.

YNYS ENLLI

8

Castellmarch, Caernarfonshire

Castellmarch, an old farm-house near Aber-soch in Llŷn, is linked to an international and onomastic tale (a tale which explains the meaning of a name). It was here, tradition tells us, that king March ap Meirchion lived. He had horse's ears (*march* is the Welsh for horse), but no-one knew except his barber. According to the earliest version of the story (recorded during the mid-sixteenth century in one of the Peniarth manuscripts, no. 134) the king had warned his barber, on pain of death, not to disclose the secret to a soul. In time, however, with the burden of the knowledge weighing heavily upon him, he sought the advice of a physician who told him to whisper his secret to the earth. This he did, and after a while fine reeds sprang up at the spot. One day the pipe-players of king Maelgwn Gwynedd passed by on their way to entertain at Castellmarch. One of the musicians cut a reed to make a new pipe, but when he played before the king the pipe would give no other sound than: 'March ap Meirchion has horse's ears'. From that day on the king never again attempted to conceal from his people the secret of his strange ears.

According to a later version of the tale (first recorded by the scholar Edward Lhuyd, 1660–1709), March used to kill each barber and bury the body where the fine reeds grew, his crime subsequently being exposed in a similar manner to that noted.

The king of Castellmarch in the Welsh versions can probably be identified with March ap Meirchion, one of King Arthur's knights, and is described in the Triads as one of the 'Three seafarers of the Island of Britain'. Midas is the king's name in the well-known story from Greek mythology. In the Cornish version the king's name is Mark, and in the Breton versions the name is Porzmarc'h and Guivarc'h. All the tales are based on folk memory of the horse's ancient reputation as a sacred animal.

9

Borth-y-gest, Caernarfonshire

The farmhouse Y Garreg Wen is situated near the sea at Borth-y-gest. It was the birth-place of David Owen, 'Dafydd y Garreg Wen' (1711/12–1741), the famous harpist and subject of many traditions. He began playing the harp when he was a very young lad at *nosweithiau llawen* ('merry evenings') in the locality. He was on his way home one evening from Plas y Borth when he laid down with his harp to rest near a large stone. In the early morning he heard the lark singing, and it was then, it is said, that he composed the tune 'Codiad yr Ehedydd' ('the rising of the lark').

He died when he was twenty nine years of age. On his death-bed one day he woke from a deep sleep and asked his mother to bring him his harp because he had dreamt that he was in heaven listening, in the company of two doves, to the most enchanting music. This, according to legend, was how the popular and melancholy air 'Dafydd y Garreg Wen' ('David of the white rock') was composed. He asked his mother to ensure that it was sung at his funeral, and this his family and friends did, all the way from his home to the cemetery of Ynys Cynhaearn Church. Two doves followed the funeral procession. Many years later, Ellis Owen (1789–1868), Cefnymeysydd, the antiquary, arranged for a memorial stone to be placed on the young harpist's grave. A harp is carved on the stone with an *englyn* (short stanza) composed by Ellis Owen.

The two tunes 'Codiad yr Ehedydd' and 'Dafydd y Garreg Wen' were first published by Edward Jones in his *Musical and Poetical Relicks of the Welsh Bards*, 1784, and at a later date the poet John Ceiriog Hughes composed Welsh words to the tunes.

10

Beddgelert, Caernarfonshire

Prince Llywelyn the Great had a favourite hound called Gelert. It was the gift of King John, father of Joan, his wife. When Llywelyn returned to his castle one day he was surprised to see Gelert running out to meet him, covered with blood. Llywelyn had a one year old son with whom Gelert used to play, and a terrible thought crossed the Prince's mind. He rushed towards the child's nursery and saw that the cradle was overturned and the room disordered and covered with blood. He looked for his son everywhere, until at last he felt sure that the dog had killed his child. In a fit of anger and rashness he plunged his sword through Gelert's heart. As the dog uttered its death-cry, a child's cry answered it from beneath the cradle. And there Llywelyn found his little son unharmed, but beside him lay the body of a huge wolf torn to pieces. Long did Llywelyn mourn the death of his faithful hound which had slain the wolf and saved the life of his heir. He buried Gelert outside the castle walls within sight of Snowdon, where every passer-by might see his grave, and raised over it a great cairn of stones. And to this day the place is called Beddgelert ('Gelert's grave').

This onomastic tale of Llywelyn's faithful hound is one of the most universally known in Wales, and thousands of people every year visit the beautiful village of Beddgelert to see the grave. Just over two hundred years ago, however, Gelert's grave did not exist. The tale of 'the man who killed his dog' is international, probably of eastern origin, and is much earlier than the time of Llywelyn the Great (1173–1240). It was also the subject of a Welsh proverb: 'As foolish as the man who slew his greyhound'.

Around 1793 David Pritchard, who had a keen eye for business, came to live at Beddgelert, from South Wales. He knew the tale of 'the man who killed his dog' and adapted it to the village of his adoption. He created the name Gelert, and Llywelyn was introduced into the story because of the Prince's connections with the old Augustinian Abbey in the locality. It was David Pritchard, with the help of the parish clerk, who erected Gelert's grave. He too, it is believed, told the story to the poet Spencer who through his ballad was the first to make the Gelert tale known to the English world. By 1800 David Pritchard had become first landlord of the new Royal Goat Hotel, which ever since has accommodated some of the many visitors to Beddgelert, a name which was originally written Beddcelert, Beddcilart or Bethcelert. Celert is possibly the name of an Irish saint or an early Celtic warrior.

11

Dinas Emrys, Caernarfonshire

Dinas Emrys is an Iron Age hill-fort opposite Llyn Dinas, between Beddgelert and Nant Gwynant. The complex early traditions relating to this fort (first mentioned by Nennius(?) in his *Historia Brittonum*, *c.* 800, and later in the tale *Cyfranc Lludd a Llefelys* in the Mabinogion) explain why the Red Dragon was adopted by the Welsh as a national emblem.

When the fifth-century British King Gwrtheyrn (Vortigern) had betrayed his own people to the Saxons he fled from his enemies to Snowdonia. There he attempted to build his own castle, but all the builders' work was mysteriously removed during the night. His magicians told him that he must find a boy born of a virgin. The boy was to be sacrificed and his blood sprinkled on the foundations. Such a boy was eventually found and his name was Emrys Wledig (Myrddin Emrys or Merlinus Ambrosius), later identified by Geoffrey of Monmouth as Myrddin (Merlin), the poet-magician. But the boy proved to be a better magician than Gwrtheyrn's. He told the king that beneath the fort's foundation was a subterranean lake in which two dragons lay sleeping, a white one representing the Saxons and a red one representing the Britons. The lake was drained and two dragons began to fight, the red one emerging victor. Gwrtheyrn was then forced to leave and he went to Nant Gwrtheyrn to build his castle. (See item 5.) The young magician built his own fort where the dragons had been fighting and it was henceforth called Dinas Emrys ('the fort of Emrys').

The Red Dragon, it is claimed, first appeared on a crest borne by King Arthur. During the Middle Ages the dragon was often referred to by Welsh poets as a symbol of the bravery of their leaders. Between 1485 and 1603 it was included as part of the arms of the Tudor dynasty. Although the Red Dragon reappeared as the royal badge of Wales in 1807, it was not until 1959, on the suggestion of the Gorsedd of the Bards, that Queen Elizabeth officially recognized it. The motto '*Y Ddraig Goch ddyry gychwyn*' ('the Red Dragon will show the way') was added to the royal badge in 1953. The words appear in a poem by Deio ab Ieuan Ddu thanking Siôn ap Rhys of Glyn-nedd (Neath) for the gift of a bull.

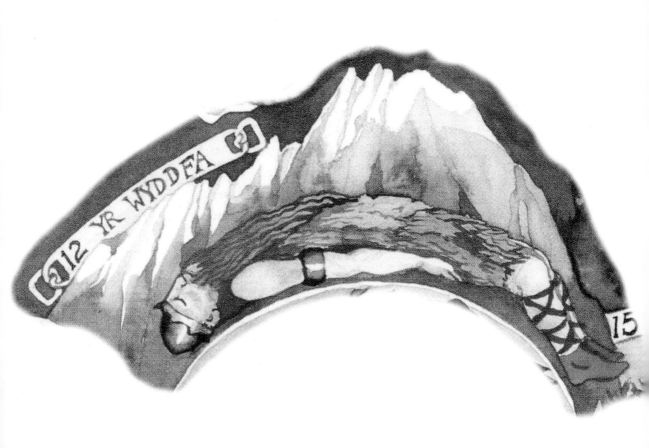

12

Yr Wyddfa (Snowdon), Caernarfonshire

There are many legends and traditions connected with Snowdon, the highest mountain in Wales (3560 feet). For example, *Eryrod Eryri*, 'the eagles of Snowdon', were long regarded as oracles of peace or war, triumph or disaster. When they circled high in the sky, victory was near, but when they flew low over the rocks, the Welsh would be defeated. It was said, too, that if they cried incessantly, the birds were mourning some impending calamity.

According to one legend the name of the mountain in former days was not Yr Wyddfa but Gwyddfa Rhita ('Rhita's cairn'). Rhita was a giant who attacked travellers and killed kings. He cut off their beards and wore them on his long mantle. He was eventually killed by Idris, a giant who lived on Cadair Idris, a mountain near Dolgellau. According to another version of the legend Rhita issued the ultimate challenge – to King Arthur himself. And he regretted it. Arthur was victorious and Rhita was buried under a large stone on Tan y Bwlch farm, Llanuwchllyn. Another tradition, on the other hand, claims that Rhita was buried in Snowdonia. Arthur ordered each one of his soldiers to place a stone over his colossal body. And that is how, it is said, the mountain of Snowdon was formed and called Gwyddfa Rhita.

13

Conwy, Caernarfonshire

A mermaid was once washed ashore by a storm on the rocks near Conwy. She begged the fishermen who found her to help her back into the sea, but they refused even to put her tail in the water and she died of exposure. A local rhyme describes vividly her cruel death.

The mermaid on the sea shore,
She cried, she screamed terribly.
There was fear of a storm the following day;
The weather was cold and she froze. (Translation)

Before she died the mermaid cursed the people of Conwy, swearing that they would always be poor. Some people believe that the curse was fulfilled. When, for example, a stranger would visit Conwy with a gold sovereign, it is said that the inhabitants had to cross over to Llansanffraid Glan Conwy to get change.

Another legend tells of a severe fish famine at Conwy. Saint Bride (Ffraid) was one day walking along the banks of the River Conwy from Llansanffraid Glan Conwy and she was throwing rushes into the water. She prayed that there would be an end to the famine, and in a few days the rushes were transformed into fish. Soon the river was teeming with the miraculous fish, which ever since have been known as *brwyniaid* ('sparlings'), meaning 'rush-like'. It is a small, tasty fish (*Osmerus eperlanus*), belonging to the same family as the trout and is comparatively rare in Britain.

14

Ffynnon Eilian, Denbighshire

Ffynnon Eilian in Llaneilian-yn-Rhos, near Colwyn Bay, was once the most famous cursing well in Wales. Saint Eilian was walking in the district one day and was afflicted by a great thirst which was quenched by drinking from a spring that sprang miraculously from the earth under his feet. He blessed its water, and God answered his prayer that the wishes of all believers who drank of its water should be granted.

Centuries later, and especially during the eighteenth and the first half of the nineteenth century, the well was misused and people from far and near visited it for the purpose of cursing and bewitching. This usually took the form of a special ceremony. The person (or persons) to be bewitched had to be placed in the well. The owner or keeper read certain passages from the Bible, he gave water from the well for the avenger to drink and sprinkled some of it over him. This was done three times while the avenger uttered his curse. The next step was to write the name of the person to be bewitched on a piece of paper, pierce it with a pin, attach the paper to a pebble and throw it into the well. This could also be done with a stone on which the victim's name was carved or with a pierced wax, clay or dough image. The name of the victim would then normally be written in the owner's book and pierced with a pin. Corks, pierced with pins, were also thrown into the water.

Before long the bewitched person would hear of the curse and hurry to the well to have his (or her) name removed from the book. He was expected to read two psalms or they would be read to him by the owner. Then he had to walk three times around the well, while still reading sections of the Bible. If his name was carved on a stone or if there was an image made of him, the well was emptied and the stone or image removed and given to him to keep. After returning home he was expected to read further sections from the Bible – often from the Book of Job and the Psalms – and sometimes for three Fridays in succession.

The owner of the well took full advantage of the superstition rife in the period and received large sums of money from both curser and cursed. It is said that Sarah Hughes received as much as £300 a year. For a period the well was in the possession of the Holland family, Cefn y Ffynnon, before it passed into the possession of the most famous of all the owners, the notorious John Evans, better known as 'Jac Ffynnon Eilian' who had the well piped into his garden. Many tales are told about him. In 1831 he was imprisoned for receiving money illegally and later, following his religious conversion, he confessed that all his activities were based on deceit. He died in 1854, and thereafter the well was no longer used for cursing. However, the saying *'fel Ffynnon Eilian'* ('like Eilian's Well') was still in use years later to convey extreme commotion or trouble.

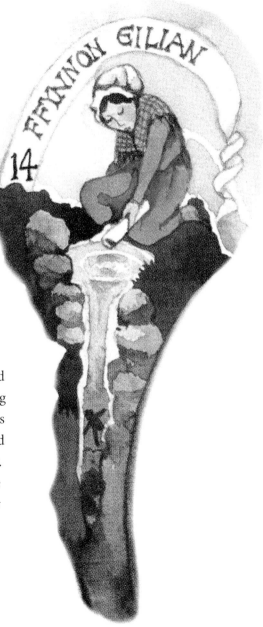

15

Llanefydd, Denbighshire

The old mansion of Berain, Llanefydd, now a farmhouse, was once the home of one of the most wealthy and influential sixteenth-century women in Wales. She was a patron of poets and noted for her beauty. Her name was Katheryn Tudur, better known as Katheryn of Berain (*c.* 1534/5–91). She married four times, and all her husbands belonged to some of the most important families in North Wales during the Elizabethan era. She had six children, and her descendants were so numerous that she is often referred to now as 'Mam Cymru', 'The Mother of Wales'.

Many years after Katheryn's death a number of legends were linked to her. It was alleged that she had seven or eight husbands and that she killed them by pouring molten lead down their ears and buried them in the orchard at Berain. According to another legend Katheryn once attacked her second husband, Sir Richard Clough, in the bedroom at Berain known as *Llofft y Marchog* ('the knight's bedroom'). His blood spattered over the wall and is supposedly irremovable. The old international tale of 'the wooer who came too late' (first printed in English in the early book *A Hundred Merry Tales*, 1526), was also connected with Katheryn. At the funeral of her first husband, John Salesbury, Lleweni, Denbigh, it is said that she was led out of church by Maurice Wyn of Gwydir, Llanrwst, who asked for her hand in marriage. Katheryn politely replied that she had already promised that honour to Sir Richard Clough, Denbigh, on the way to the funeral, but she added: if the same sad misfortune should befall her second husband, he could rely on being her third. And so it was. Maurice Wyn became her third husband. Katheryn died in 1591 and was buried at Llanefydd churchyard. Edward Thelwal, Plas y Ward, Ruthin, her fourth husband, survived her.

The illustration published in this book is based on a portrait of Katheryn, painted in 1568 by a Dutch artist [Adriaen van Cronenburgh?], while Katheryn and Sir Richard Clough were living in Antwerp. The painting hangs in the National Museum of Wales. Her right hand is holding the Book of Common Prayer or a little casket which, according to one tradition, contains a lock of Sir Richard Clough's hair. The left hand is resting on a human skull – a reminder of life's brevity (*memento mori*).

16

Treffynnon (Holywell), Flintshire

Saint Winifred's Well (Ffynnon Gwenfrewi), the most famous holy well in Wales, is situated on the right hand side of the road leading from Holywell to Maes-glas (Greenfield). From the Middle Ages until the present day pilgrims and the sick from near and far have visited this well to be blessed or cured by its cold, crystal-clear water. It is referred to as one of the 'Seven Wonders of Wales', and is said to have miraculous healing properties, especially for nervous disorders.

Winifred, who lived in the seventh century and had dedicated her life to serve God, was a very beautiful daughter of a noble family. According to tradition, Gwenlo, her mother, was Saint Beuno's sister, and it was he who instructed her in the Christian faith. A young spirited chieftain called Caradog fell in love with Winifred, but she would have nothing to do with him. In his anger Caradog beheaded her with his sword at a place called Sychnant, near Holywell. The head rolled down a hill towards Beuno's chapel and at the exact spot where it stopped a well of clear water sprang from the ground. Beuno restored Winifred's head to her body and revived her, the only trace of her traumatic experience being a narrow white line where head and body were reunited.

Later a chapel was built around the well. Tiny red pebbles were discovered nearby and it was said that they had been stained by Saint Winifred's blood.

Winifred stayed for seven years at Holywell, assisting Beuno, her uncle. Then she went to live with Saint Eleri in a convent at Gwytherin, Clwyd, where she died. There are two days in the Calendar of the Saints which commemorate Saint Winifred: 22 June commemorates her martyrdom and 3 November commemorates her second death.

When Saint Beuno saw Caradog's misdeed he cursed him there and then. The earth

opened under his feet and swallowed him. It is also said that God's vengeance descended upon Caradog's descendants. They barked like dogs and could not be cured until they had washed their bodies in Saint Winifred's Well or visited her grave at Shrewsbury Monastery, where Saint Winifred's remains were re-buried in 1138.

17

Rhuthun, Denbighshire

Huail son of Caw was reputedly ruler of Edeirnion in North Wales and a brother of Gildas, the sixth-century monk and historian, author of *De Excidio Britanniae* ('On the Destruction of Britain'). Gildas loved and obeyed Arthur, king of all Britain, but his twenty three brothers were his enemies. Huail, the eldest, was the most disobedient of them all.

According to the Mabinogion tale of Culhwch and Olwen, Huail stabbed his nephew, Gwydre fab Llwydeu, thereby kindling the wrath of Arthur. The Life of Gildas, written by Caradog of Llancarfan, claims that Arthur killed Huail, and Giraldus Cambrensis in his *Descriptio Kambriae* (*c*. 1194) repeats the allegation. He further adds that Gildas was so aggrieved that he threw all the books he had written about Arthur's exploits into the sea.

A later version of the tradition concerning the animosity between Arthur and Huail was recorded by Elis Gruffydd, 'The Soldier of Calais' (*c*. 1490–*c*. 1552) in his Chronicle. Huail stole one of Arthur's mistresses and in a fight which followed Arthur was wounded in the knee. He agreed to forgive Huail on condition that he would never mention the wound. Shortly afterwards Arthur disguised himself as a woman and secretly left his court at Caerwys in Clwyd and went to Ruthin where his mistress was attending a dance. Huail recognised Arthur by his limp and remarked: 'Your dancing would be fine but for your lame knee.' For this remark Arthur punished Huail by beheading him on a large stone, now called maen Huail ('Huail's stone'). It has been carefully preserved until this day in St. Peter's Square, Rhuthun.

18 MYNYDD HIRAETHOG

18

Mynydd Hiraethog, Denbighshire

Sioned, the daughter of Foty Tai Canol, Hafod Elwy, on the Hiraethog Mountain and Ffowc Owen, the son of Tan y Graig, Hafod Elwy, were lovers. But Ffowc Owen's family felt that Sioned, a maid at Tai Ucha nearby, was an unworthy match for a farmer's son. On the advice of his parents, therefore, young Ffowc Owen married another girl and went to live in Ty'n Gors, a farm near Tai Ucha.

He was an excellent carpenter, and one day during the winter of 1772 had gone to the village of Nantglyn to fetch some wood for making furniture. But on the return journey he was caught in a blinding snow storm and died within two fields of his new home. For three weeks the neighbours searched for his body, but to no avail.

Then Sioned, his old lover, had the same dream three nights in succession, and each time she saw Ffowc Owen cutting hay on one of the moors near Ty'n Gors and then lying down beside the mountain wall at midday to rest. Sioned finally decided to tell her mistress about her recurrent dream. The neighbours immediately went to the mountain wall to search in the snow, and there they found the frozen body of Ffowc Owen precisely where Sioned had seen him, with his cap covering his face. His sack-load of timber had already been discovered on the bridge over the Brenig river.

A cairn of white flint-stones was raised at the place where Ffowc Owen's body was found, and although it is now virtually enclosed by the Forestry Commission's plantation, one or two local people still keep the cairn of white stones tidy and clear of undergrowth.

19
Valle Crucis, Denbighshire

Valle Crucis Abbey, known in Welsh as Glyn y Groes and Glynegwestl, was founded in 1201 by the Cistercian Order. It is situated on the banks of the river Eglwyseg in the Vale of Llangollen. Until its dissolution in 1536 it was noted as a centre of culture and learning and for the generosity shown to Welsh poets such as Guto'r Glyn and Lewys Môn.

A well-known tale concerns the encounter of one of the abbots of Valle Crucis with Owain Glyndŵr (c. 1354–c. 1416), Prince of Wales and national hero. Owain had two homes not far from Llangollen, one at Carrog and one at Sycharth, near Llansilin on the English border. From about the year 1400 onwards Owain Glyndŵr was recognised by the Welsh people as their undisputed leader in their fight against English dominance. By 1406, the military power of the English Crown was reasserting itself, and by 1413 the Welsh uprising had finally been suppressed. From that time onwards the Welsh Prince simply disappeared from the historical scene and his whereabouts were unknown. There is no definite information even about the date, place or manner of his death, but he was never betrayed, and his name has remained a source of inspiration to Welsh people.

There is a tradition that Owain Glyndŵr, like King Arthur, is still alive and will return again one day to lead his men to freedom. A tale, recorded by the chronicler Elis Gruffydd, 'The Soldier of Calais', relates how the Abbot of Valle Crucis early one morning met him walking alone on the Berwyn hills. 'You have risen early, Master Abbot', said the Prince, to which the Abbot replied: 'No, my Lord, it is you who have risen early – a hundred years too early.' And thereupon Owain walked away and disappeared in the morning mist.

19 VALLE CRUCIS

20

Llangar, Sir Feirionnydd

The historical church of Llangar is situated one mile from the town of Corwen and one mile from the village of Cynwyd. According to a well-known local tradition it was first attempted to build the church on a small hill near where, today, the bridge at Cynwyd crosses the River Dee. But however hard the masons worked during the day the stones were mysteriously removed during the night. Who or what was responsible nobody knew. The builders went to seek the advice of a wise man who told them: 'God is unwilling for you to build your church here, you must hunt the White Stag (*Carw Gwyn*) and wherever you raise the stag, there you must build the church.'

This they did. The White Stag was raised at the precise spot where Llangar's Church of All Saints stands today. It is said that the church's original name was Llan-garw-gwyn ('the church of the white stag'). This name was shortened eventually to Llan-garw and finally to Llangar. A local rhyme recounts the story of the hunt and attempts to explain the meaning of local place-names:

> *It was raised at Llangar;*
> *It was killed at Moel Lladdfa*
> ('the moor of slaughter');
> *It was buried* (hidden) *at Fronguddio*
> ('the hill of hiding');
> *It decayed at Y Bedren*
> ('the place of decay'). (Translation)

Local legends similar to the above are told of many churches in Wales. Their specific function is to explain the location of the present church or, occasionally, the meaning of a name connected with the church. (There is a strong onomastic element, although there is usually no etymological foundation for the meaning suggested.) The prime function of the legends, however, is to emphasize the triumph of good over evil. The evil spirit, or the Devil, opposes the building of the church, and the White Stag symbolizes the purity and triumphant goodness of God.

20 LLANGAR

21

Llyn Tegid (Bala Lake), Merionethshire

There was once a cruel and infamous prince who terrorised his people. His name was Tegid Foel and he lived in the old town of Bala. (See also item 27.) One day he heard a voice saying: '*Dial a ddaw, dial a ddaw*.' ('Vengeance will come, vengeance will come.')

He heard the voice day after day, but each time he mocked and laughed the threat away. One evening there was great rejoicing at the birth of the first child of the Prince's son and a young, poor harpist from the neighbouring hills was invited to come to the palace to entertain. During an interval at midnight he heard a voice whispering in his ear: '*Dial a ddaeth, dial a ddaeth*.' ('Vengeance has come, vengeance has come.')

Then he saw a small bird beckoning him to leave the palace. This he did and followed the bird to the hills, where he rested until the following morning. But at the break of dawn not a single stone of the old town of Bala was in sight, only a large lake with his harp floating on the waters. And the lake has been known ever since as Llyn Tegid.

An earlier and less familiar legend relates how the lake was formed when the guardian of a well, known as Ffynnon Gywer, forgot one night to replace the lid. (Llangywer today is the name of a village and parish near the lake.)

A popular local rhyme incorporates the prophecy that the present town of Bala, too, one day will be drowned and that the water will extend as far as the village of Llanfor. (A popular meaning for Llanfor is given as: *llan* (church) + *môr* (sea).)

> *Y Bala aeth a'r Bala aiff,*
> *A Llanfor aiff yn llyn.*

('Bala has gone (drowned) and Bala will drown again,
And Llanfor will become a lake.)

Another local legend relating to Llyn Tegid refers to an eighteenth-century harpist, known as 'Charles y Telynor' ('Charles the harpist'), from Llanycil Parish. It was believed, especially by religious people, that he had sold his soul to the Devil by offering Communion bread to dogs. He did everything to mock and hinder the work of the early Welsh Nonconformists – Howel Harris, for example, who suffered his wrath in an interlude. But on the way home with his harp late one evening after playing in a *noson lawen* at Fach Ddeiliog (a farmhouse) he drowned in Bala Lake and a cloud of smoke was seen rising above the spot where he sank.

22 PENNANT MELANGELL

22

Pennant Melangell, Montgomeryshire

Brochwel Ysgythrog, a sixth-century prince of Powys, was one day out hunting in the district of Pennant between the Berwyn mountain and the present Lake Efyrnwy in the former county of Montgomery. A hare ran in front of him and took refuge between the feet of a beautiful young maiden. The Prince urged his hounds to catch the hare, but they were afraid to approach her. The young maiden, too, begged him not to kill it. One of the huntsmen raised his horn to call the dogs again, but not a single note issued from it and it stuck to his lips. Bewildered by these strange events, Brochwel asked the maiden's name who told him that she was Melangell (Monacella) who had fled from Ireland to avoid marrying an Irish chieftain against her will. She came to Wales to worship God in the peace and beauty of Pennant. The Prince, realising that he was in the presence of a holy person, gave her land to build a chapel. And there she remained throughout her life in the service of God.

Melangell's encounter with Brochwel is illustrated in wood carvings on the screen of the beautiful Norman church at Pennant Melangell. Her alleged stone bed and tomb are also said to be near the church. She became the patron saint of hares, and in Pennant and the surrounding districts hares are even to this day sometimes called *ŵyn bach Melangell* ('Melangell's little lambs'). It was also once considered unlucky to kill a hare.

23

Mawddwy, Merionethshire

Gwylliaid Cochion Mawddwy ('the Red Bandits of Mawddwy'), were a notorious band of outlaws who terrorised the districts around Dinas Mawddwy and Mallwyd during the fifteenth and sixteenth centuries. Until the nineteenth century there were houses in the area with scythe blades lodged in the chimneys, said to have been placed there centuries earlier to protect the occupants from the outlaws. In the mid-sixteenth century many of them were captured. One tradition states that Baron Lewis Owen (High Sheriff of Merioneth, 1554–5) condemned over eighty to die on Christmas Eve 1554 at a place where a house called Collfryn ('the hill of loss') stands today. They were buried in a mound which may still be seen on nearby land known as Rhos Goch ('the red or bloody moor'), about two miles east of the village of Mallwyd.

Another tradition states that the mother of two of the outlaws pleaded in vain to Baron Owen to spare the life of at least her youngest son. Then, baring her bosom, she cursed him and said: 'These breasts have nurtured other sons who will wash their hands in your heart's blood.' In 1555, less than a year later, Baron Owen was murdered by the outlaws in Dugoed Mawddwy at a place near Collfryn known ever since as Llidiart y Barwn ('the baron's gate'). (He was on his way home to Dolgellau from the Assizes at Welshpool.) One tradition asserts that the murderers, remembering their mother's curse, returned to the scene of the murder to wash their hands in the blood from Baron Owen's heart.

Among the many other places in Mawddwy traditionally associated with the *Gwylliaid* are farms in Cwm Dugoed, a cemetery (Mynwent y Gwylliaid), a bridge (Pont y Lladron, 'the bridge of the thieves'), a ford (Sarn y Gwylliaid), a well (Ffynnon y Gwylliaid), and a ravine (Ceunant y Gwylliaid).

It is believed that all the male members of the clan were executed following the murder of Lewis Owen. Yet, people with red hair in parts of Merioneth and Montgomery today are still sometimes jokingly alluded to as descendants of the 'Red Bandits of Mawddwy'.

24 NANNAU

24

Nannau, Merionethshire

For centuries Nannau, near Dolgellau, Merioneth, has been the home of a noble family which claims descent from the princes of Powys through Ynyr Hen. Nannau (and Nanney) was also for a time the family's surname, but in the eighteenth century it changed to Vaughan through the marriage of Sioned Nanney and Robert Vaughan of Hengwrt. The family were patrons of poets and played an important role in the political life of the county of Merioneth.

The Lord of Nannau at the beginning of the fifteenth century was Hywel Sele. According to tradition he was a cousin of Owain Glyndŵr, but they were not on good terms. The Abbot of Cymer tried to reconcile the two men and Owain was invited to Nannau.

One day they were out hunting deer when, without warning, Hywel shot an arrow at Owain's heart. The murderous act was foiled by the armour underneath Owain's tunic and both men fell upon each other. Hywel was killed and his body hidden inside a hollow oak tree at Nannau. The body remained there, undiscovered for many years, and the tree became known as *Ceubren yr Ellyll* ('the demon's hollow tree').

25

Egryn, Merionethshire

During the fervour of religious revivals, such as the 1904–5 Revival in Wales, many people have witnessed strange lights in the sky and heard the pleasant sound of hymn-singing. Nowhere in Wales, however, was this paranormal phenomenon more noted than in the small hamlet of Egryn on the road between Harlech and Barmouth, Dyffryn Ardudwy, during the year 1905.

The focus of attention was the tiny Egryn Chapel and one of its members, thirty five year old Mrs Mary Jones, a woman of strong psychic tendencies who lived at Is-law'r Ffordd farm. During the first stirrings of the Revival in South Wales, and especially under the influence of Evan Roberts's inspired preaching, she became the subject of a dramatic conversion. Not long after returning to North Wales she began to experience regular visions. She would be surrounded by moving lights and would receive messages from 'the Saviour in bodily form'. She believed she had been chosen as God's instrument to spread the Revival in Merioneth.

When she began her own nightly services at Egryn Chapel she soon became famous for her visionary preaching, and people from far and near, including newspaper journalists, came to listen to her and especially to witness the mysterious lights which would appear over and in the chapel. Usually the lights took the form of a luminous arch, similar to the *aurora borealis*, with one end resting in the sea and the other on a hilltop, about a mile away. This would be followed soon after by a 'star' which filled the chapel with soft light. Once a train was moving slowly past Pen-sarn Chapel where Mrs Jones was preaching when the driver (a Machynlleth man) saw strange lights shooting out from ten different directions and subsequently meeting with a crack. Often Mrs Jones's 'star' would be seen hovering over a specific house and this usually signalled the conversion of one or more of the inhabitants.

As the fervour of the Revival gradually subsided, the mysterious Egryn lights, too, disappeared and no one has witnessed them ever since.

26

Aberdyfi, Merionethshire

I n the upland country behind Aberdyfi there is a mountain lake called Llyn Barfog ('the bearded lake'). One tradition claims that this is the bottomless lake referred to in the Welsh Triads as Llyn Llion whose banks were broken by the great water monster *Yr Afanc* causing the inundation of the surrounding land. The recurrence of the catastrophe was prevented only through the intervention of Hu Gadarn (Hu the Mighty) who, assisted by the *Ychen Bannog* (the 'long horned oxen'), dragged the *Afanc* out of the lake.

Another tradition links Llyn Barfog with the abode of Gwyn ap Nudd, King of the Fairies and Lord of the Underworld. *Gwragedd Annwfn* ('women of the Underworld'), attired in green, were said to have been seen by the banks of the lake with their herd of noble, white cattle which gave a never-ending supply of rich, creamy milk.

A popular local legend relates how a neighbouring farmer was fortunate enough to acquire one of these remarkable cows. She was known as *Y Fuwch Gyfeiliorn* ('the stray cow'). (Other names for her in legends from Wales and elsewhere connected with various lakes are: The Fairy Cow, The Dun Cow, The Mystic Cow, The Holy Cow, and *Y Fuwch Laethwen Lefrith* ('the milk-white cow'). Soon the cow became the wonder of the neighbourhood. Never had anyone seen such milk and such calves. His incomparable herd made the farmer a very wealthy man. But wealth also made him proud, and his pride made him forget his obligation to the stray cow. He was afraid that in ageing she would become unprofitable, and he fattened her ready for the butcher. The day of the slaughter came and all the farmers in the locality gathered to see the, by now, monstrously fat cow. But when the butcher raised his arm to strike the fatal blow, it was paralysed and the knife fell from his hand. A piercing cry was heard, and a lady in pale green robes appeared above Llyn Barfog, calling in a loud clear voice:

> *Come thou, Einion's Yellow One,*
> *Stray-horns, the Speckled Cow of the Lake,*
> *And the Hornless Dodin,*
> *Arise, come home. (Translation)*

And thereupon, the Stray Cow and all her progeny, to the third and fourth generations, left the farm and disappeared for ever into the lake.

27

Tre Taliesin, Ceredigion

Tre Taliesin (formerly known as Comins y Dafarn Fach) is a village between Machynlleth and Aberystwyth. It was given its present name in the 1820s because of its alleged connection with Taliesin, the sixth-century court poet. *Bedd Taliesin*, Taliesin's reputed grave, is one mile east of the village alongside a rough track from Pen-sarn-ddu farm. He became a figure of the utmost importance in Celtic myth, and his name in the fields of poetry and art is synonymous with inspiration and continuity. Though a native of Powys, he resided for much of his life during the second half of the sixth century in the Old North (Southern Scotland and Northern England) and wrote poems in praise of Urien and his son Owain, princes of Rheged, the present counties of Wigtown and Kirkcudbright. (His poetry, and that of Aneirin, is the earliest in the Welsh language.)

Later a wide range of prophetic, legendary and religious poetry (written mainly during the ninth and tenth century) was also attributed to Taliesin and written down in a manuscript known as *Llyfr Taliesin* (The Book of Taliesin), c. 1275. By that time a highly amusing legend had grown up around him which must have formed an essential part of the repertoire of medieval storytellers. It explains vividly the circumstances of his birth and the source of his magical powers.

Tegid Foel had a wife called Ceridwen. (See also item 21.) She was a witch and had the ugliest son in the world, Morfran, also known as *Afagddu*, 'the blackest one of all'. For one year and a day she boiled potent herbs in a cauldron. At the end of that time Morfran was to swallow the three remaining drops thus acquiring ultimate power, knowledge and beauty. But the sacred drops were accidentally swallowed by a young lad called Gwion Bach who fled in fear of Ceridwen's wrath. Ceridwen gave chase and Gwion turned into a hare. The witch in turn became a greyhound. When Gwion transformed himself into a fish, Ceridwen became an otter. When he became a bird, she hunted him as a hawk. Finally, Gwion became a grain of wheat, but Ceridwen turned into a hen and swallowed him. In nine months time she gave birth to a son, but the child was so beautiful that she could not destroy him. She sewed him up in a skin bag and cast him adrift in the sea in a coracle.

The bag was found on May Eve by Elffin at Cored Wyddno ('Gwyddno Weir'), on the edge of the Mochno bog, near where the village of Borth is today. Marvelling at his lovely forhead (*tal*), Elffin called the baby Taliesin ('beautiful brow'). Elffin was the son of Gwyddno Garanhir, King of Maes Gwyddno, or Cantre'r Gwaelod ('the lowland hundred'), where Taliesin was brought up. When it was drowned by the sea Taliesin escaped. (See item 34.)

28

Dylife, Montgomeryshire

Today Dylife is a small, quiet village near the Clywedog Reservoir, but once it was a busy lead-mining centre. It was also the scene of one of the most horrific murders in Welsh history.

Sometime during the beginning of the eighteenth century a man, believed to be from Ceredigion, came to work in the mines at Dylife. His name was John Jones, 'Siôn y Gof' ('Siôn the blacksmith'). Later his wife, Catherine David (from Llanfihangel-y-Creuddyn?) and her two children, Thomas Lloyd and Avarina Lloyd, travelled to Dylife to visit him and, possibly, to set up residence there. But a dispute arose. The blacksmith threw his family down one of the lead pits at three o'clock in the afternoon on 23 October (1719?). Their bodies were not discovered until the 9 January (1720?). Siôn was courting with a maid-servant from Dylife at the time of the murder and when asked what had driven him to commit such a horrific crime is said to have replied: 'Because of some other woman and the Devil.' According to one tradition he threw his family down the mine because he believed that the end of the world was near. There is also a tradition that one of the children, before dying, had 'eaten its mother's breast'.

Siôn y Gof was hanged near the pit on a hill known afterwards as Pen y Grocbren ('gallows hill'). His body was then gibbetted, that is, placed in an iron frame and left out in the weather to rot in full view of all. In 1938 his skull and the iron frame surrounding it was discovered. It is now in the open-air museum at St. Fagans.

Ballads were composed to commemorate the murder and a few lines from these may still be heard today in oral tradition, especially the following (translated from the Welsh):

Siôn y Gof on an auburn mare
Went to be hanged above Dylife.

People in the area also refer to Llyn Siôn y Gof ('Siôn y Gof's lake) in the River Clywedog, a piece of Siôn y Gof's bed; Siôn y Gof's Ghost (a headless man); and the Ghost of Siôn y Gof's Wife.

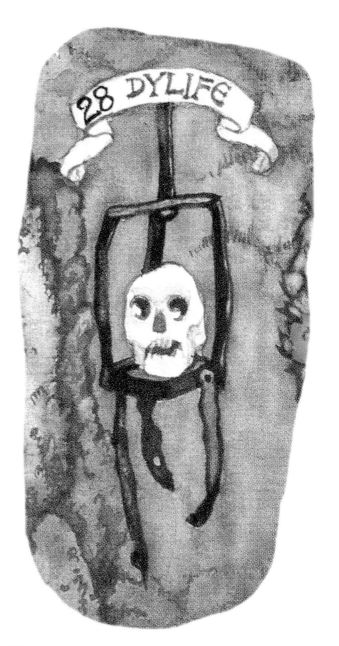

29

Llanllwchaearn, Montgomeryshire

Henry Williams (1624–84) owned the farm of Ysgafell in the parish of Llanllwchaearn, near Newtown. He became a follower of the great Puritan leader Vavasor Powell (1617–70) and, as in the case of many of the early Nonconformists, he suffered severe persecution. He was once attacked while preaching and almost killed. Following the Restoration of the Monarchy in 1660 he spent a total of nine years in prison. During those years his furniture and farm stock were either stolen or destroyed and his house was burnt to the ground.

When everything seemed to have been lost and his family were on the verge of starvation, fate intervened. Wheat sowed in a field near the house grew prolifically and astonished the whole country. From that time Henry Williams and his family suffered no more poverty. Many of the thieves who had stolen his property were said to have died suddenly; his persecutors were struck with fear and he was allowed to live the rest of his life in peace.

The field where the marvellous wheat had grown is called *Cae'r Fendith* ('the field of blessing') to this day. Two ears of wheat of the rivet variety, said to have come from this field, were carefully preserved by the family from one generation to the next. They are now deposited at St. Fagans.

30
TREFALDWYN

30

Trefaldwyn, Montgomeryshire

About the year 1819 the wealthy widow of James Morris, Oakfield Farm, near Montgomery appointed a man named John Newton as bailiff. He was an excellent worker and soon the farm was flourishing under his care. By becoming friendly with Mrs Morris's daughter, however, Newton unwittingly incurred the enmity of two men. One, Robert Parker, wanted the farm for himself, while the other, Thomas Pearce, wanted to marry the girl.

One day in November 1821 the bailiff had gone to Welshpool and had stayed there rather late before returning home. That evening Parker and Pearce committed a robbery and made it appear as though Newton was the thief. John Newton was tried and condemned to death. On the scaffold he cursed his accusers and swore that his innocence would be proved by the fact that nothing would grow on his grave for at least one generation.

Thirty years after the bailiff's death there was still a bare patch on his grave, which is known as 'The Robber's Grave', and is in the churchyard at Montgomery. Soon after the hanging, Thomas Pearce became a drunkard and was killed in a quarry explosion. Robert Parker died of a wasting disease shortly afterwards. It was also considered dangerous to attempt to grow anything on the grave and there is a story that one man who planted a rose bush there suffered an untimely death.

31

Llangurig, Montgomeryshire

During the period around 1860–1940 the most renowned family of wise men in Wales lived in the Llangurig district. The term 'wise man' (in Welsh '*Y Dyn Hysbys*', lit. 'the knowing one') was once widely used in Wales to describe a person reputed to have the gift of counteracting witchcraft and dispelling evil spirits. He was also known as a conjurer, charmer and magician. There were three main kinds of wise men: clerics (for example, Edmwnd Prys); men expert in medicine and black magic (the most famous of these was Dr John Harries, Cwrtycadno); and, finally, men who had inherited their gift as members of a particular family.

The wise man or *dyn hysbys* was so called because he was a knowledgeable person and believed to be familiar with the unfamiliar. He was usually sagacious and well-read, but he also took advantage of people's fear, ignorance and superstition. His main functions were to cure and protect animals and, occasionally, people; to assist farmers who had difficulty in churning; to discover lost animals; and to dispel evil spirits (an activity usually associated with clerics). The witch had the power only to bewitch. The wise man was endowed with the power to bewitch and to dispel evil spirits.

Two well-known members of the Llangurig family of wise men were Evan Griffiths, Pant-y-benni, Llangurig, and Edward Davies, Y Fagwyr Fawr, Ponterwyd. They learned their art from other members of the family and from books. They also had a particular talent for curing animals. They won great fame, however, because so many people from north and Mid Wales visited them in the belief that they had supernatural power to cure and protect animals. In return for a sum of money the wise man wrote his charm on a piece of paper in almost illegible handwriting and in a mixture of Welsh, English and Latin. It included a prayer on behalf of the bewitched animals or a blessing to protect animals from being bewitched; the abracadabra; and, finally, various signs of the zodiac. The charm was then carefully placed inside a small bottle known as *potel y dyn hysbys*. The farmer was to take care to hide the bottle in a building where the animals were kept, and the cork was on no account to be removed.

Examples of charms written by the Llangurig wise men are kept at the National Library of Wales, and at St Fagans, where there is also an example of the wise man's bottle with a charm inside it. Another similar bottle is still carefully preserved today in a farmhouse in the Llanfair Caereinion district. The family firmly believe that the bottle should never be removed or opened because the spirit of the Squire of Bryn Glas – the evil spirit which troubled the farm – is forever imprisoned inside.

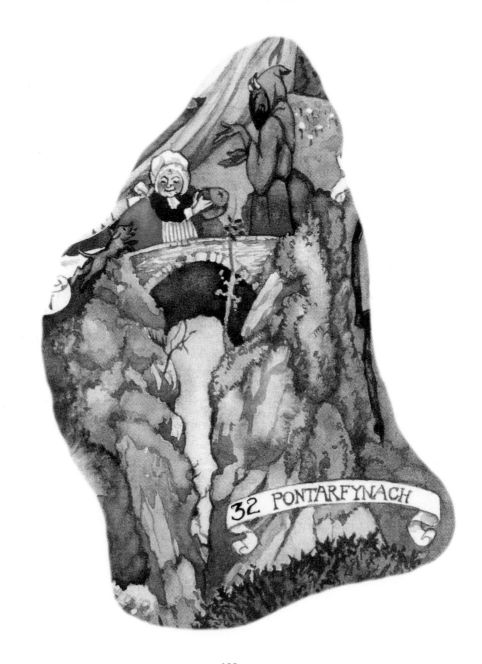

32

Pontarfynach (Devil's Bridge), Ceredigion

In Wales, as elsewhere, bridges were built over ravines so high that, according to legend, only the Devil himself could have constructed them. One such example is Aberglaslyn Bridge, near Beddgelert, Gwynedd. There was also a common belief that the Devil owned the soul of the first living creature to cross a new bridge. The best known legend in Wales is the one associated with the first of the three bridges built across the deep gorge of the River Mynach at Pontarfynach ('the bridge over the river Mynach'), or Devil's Bridge.

Many years ago an old woman, called Megan Llandunach, had lost her cow. She looked everywhere for it and eventually saw it stranded on the other side of the gorge through which the River Mynach flowed. While she was crying and bewailing her fate the Devil came along, dressed as a cloven-footed monk. He promised the old woman that he would build a bridge over the gorge on condition that he would own the soul of the first living creature to cross it. She agreed, and the bridge was built overnight. In the morning the Devil called on Megan to view the bridge and to claim his due. The old woman, however, told him that she wished first to throw a loaf of bread over the new bridge to test its strength. Megan's hungry dog ran after the bread – and the old Devil was outwitted.

33

Nanteos, Ceredigion

Nanteos is a spacious mansion near Capel Seion, about two and a half miles south-east of Aberystwyth. The present house was built in 1739 and was for many generations the home of the Powell family, descendants of Edwin ap Gronw, Lord of Tegeingl, a hundred in north-east Wales. Many celebrities, such as the poet Swinburne, visited the mansion, but its greatest claim to fame is the fact that it was the home of the sacred Nanteos Cup, a wooden bowl carefully safeguarded by the family from one generation to the next.

Some people believe that the cup was made from Christ's cross, but the belief most popularly held is that this was the cup used by Christ at the Last Supper – the Holy Grail so eagerly sought after by King Arthur's knights and the subject of so many legends during the Middle Ages. It was, according to tradition, brought to Glastonbury by Joseph of Arimathea and from there it came to Strata Florida (Ystrad-fflur). Following the Dissolution of the Monasteries in the reign of Henry VIII seven monks, we are told, brought the cup from Strata Florida to Nanteos for safe-keeping.

The cup was supposed to have miraculous healing powers and people from far afield visited Nanteos to see and touch the holy relic. One tradition asserts that Wagner visited Nanteos and was inspired by the cup to compose his opera *Parcival*, but this tradition cannot be confirmed. It is probably based on George Powell's admiration of Wagner's works.

Because of the extensive use made of the cup, only a small fragment of it still remains. It was kept in Herefordshire, still in the possession of the Powell (Mirylees) family who left Nanteos in the nineteen sixties. [Since 2016 the cup has been on permanent display at the National Library of Wales.]

34

Cantre'r Gwaelod, Ceredigion

Cantre'r Gwaelod is the name given to the land which once, according to legend, extended from Cardigan to Bardsey Island and was submerged by a sudden coastal flooding. In the earliest form of the legend, first referred to in the thirteenth century and recorded in *Llyfr Du Caerfyrddin* (The Black Book of Carmarthen), the land is called Maes Gwyddno and it was drowned when a well-maiden, named Mererid, ignored her duties. The tradition as it is known today was formed from the seventeenth century onwards and was influenced by stories from the Low Countries about the construction of dykes and dams. The submerged land of Cardigan Bay is called Cantre'r Gwaelod ('the lowland hundred'). It had sixteen noble cities, and Gwyddno Garanhir was its king. It was defended from the sea by an embankment and sluices. Seithennin was keeper of the sluices, and one evening when there was a great banquet he became drunk and left the sluices open. The water rushed in and drowned the inhabitants. The poet Taliesin was the only one to escape alive. (See item 27.) Ever since, according to the legend, some people believe that they can hear the faint music of the Cantre'r Gwaelod Church bells ringing beneath the waves. This tale is the subject of a poem by J. J. Williams, 'Clychau Cantre'r Gwaelod' ('the bells of the lowland hundred'). A well-known folk song called 'Clychau Aberdyfi' is also often associated with the bells of the sixteen noble cities which lie forever beneath the sea.

When man first came to live on the coast of Wales (sometime between the Neolithic and the Iron Age) the sea level was still rising between Wales and Ireland, separating the two countries further and further, and the legend relating to the drowning of the Lowland Hundred probably developed as a result of folk memory of a sudden coastal flooding many centuries ago.

The remains of peat and tree trunks which are visible on the beaches when the tide is far out further captured man's imagination.

Similar traditions are connected with certain Welsh lakes; for example, Llyn Tegid (Bala Lake) and Llyn Syfaddan (Llan-gorse Lake), Powys (see items 21 and 43), and with other parts of the Welsh coast, for example, Tyno Helyg and Caer Arianrhod, Gwynedd; Morfa Rhianedd, Clwyd; and Cynffig, Morgannwg. The moralistic and onomastic elements in all these traditions are very obvious. Similar traditions are to be found in other countries.

35

Pennant, Ceredigion

Mari Berllan Piter lived in the neighbourhood of Pennant, between Cross Inn and Aberaeron. She was a poor, hump-backed old woman, a recluse who was often seen wandering among the graves and who was fond of black cats and snakes. The ruins of her cottage, Perllan Piter, are now almost hidden in the midst of its overgrown orchard (*perllan*), and Mari herself has been resting in Llanbadarn Trefeglwys churchyard since 1896. Yet the numerous anecdotes and traditions told about her are very much alive in the memory of some of the inhabitants of Pennant and district today.

There was widespread belief that she had all power to bewitch, and people of all ages lived in fear of her curse. When farmers' wives failed to churn or when animals became ill, poor Mari was usually blamed. Indeed, some farmers used to give her a sack of flour, or similar gift, to ensure that she would not bewitch their animals. Once, when Dic y Felin, the miller, refused to grind her flour she caused the wheel of his mill to turn in the opposite direction. And when a young girl ventured to steal an apple from her orchard she was forced to walk backwards all the way home.

Another of Mari's alleged attributes was the power to transform herself into a rabbit or a hare. When neighbours attempted to shoot at her she fled out of sight into the chimney of her cottage. According to one belief it was not possible to shoot a hare-witch unless the bullet was made either of silver or the root of the sacred plant, black bryony (*Tamus communis*).

There is, however, no account that Mari was ever shot or wounded. Indeed, many people believe that her spirit is still alive today. People who have attempted to photograph her cottage (now called 'The Witch's Cottage') have encountered great difficulty, and when, in 1981, the Theatr Felin-fach Company were preparing a pageant based on her life story, the actors and producers experienced all kinds of problems and mishaps which were attributed to the spirit of 'Old Mari Berllan Piter'.

36

Strata Florida (Ystrad-fflur), Ceredigion

The Cistercian abbey of Strata Florida, founded 1164, was one of the most important abbeys in the country, with its lands extending over a large area of Mid Wales. A number of Welsh princes were buried here, for example, Cadell ap Gruffydd (1175) and Maelgwn ap Rhys (*c.* 1230). The abbey was a generous patron and important literary works were written there, including probably the original Latin version of *Brut y Tywysogion* (Chronicle of the Princes) towards the end of the thirteenth century. Poets, for example, Guto'r Glyn, Dafydd Nanmor and Ieuan Deulwyn, composed poems in praise of the abbey and its abbots.

It is generally believed that the celebrated poet Dafydd ap Gwilym (*fl.* 1320–70) was buried at Ystrad-fflur (and not at Talyllychau (Talley) abbey). The assertion is based on a poem written by Gruffudd Gryg which suggests that the remains of the poet were buried under a yew tree in the abbey's cemetery. According to a local belief the same yew tree is still growing in the cemetery today.

Strata Florida abbey was dissolved in 1539 during Henry VIII's reign, but for some years after tradition asserts that eternal candles were seen burning day and night amid the ruins, and on Christmas Eve the ghost of one of the monks was also seen rebuilding the altar. (See also item 39.)

37

Tregaron, Ceredigion

One of the famous men of Tregaron was Twm Siôn Cati (*c.* 1530–1609). His real name was Thomas Jones, and he was the illegitimate son of Siôn ap Dafydd ap Madog ap Hywel Moetheu of Porth-y-ffin, near Tregaron. His mother's name was Catherine (Cati). To his contemporaries Thomas Jones, no doubt, was a respectable gentleman, landlord and antiquary, noted for his talent as a herald or genealogist. Years later, however, numerous apocryphal tales were associated with his name which portray him as a notorious highwayman, outlaw and trickster. This may be explained by the fact that in 1559, during the first year of Queen Elizabeth's reign, he received an official pardon (though we are not told the nature of his crime). It is also possible that he was mistaken for other highway-robbers of the same name in the Tregaron district.

Many of the tales and anecdotes relating to Twm were recorded by T. J. Llewelyn Prichard in his popular novel *The Adventures and Vagaries of Twm Shon Catti* (1828). A Welsh version of the novel was also published later.

In some of the stories told about him he is a man to be feared. This, for example, is the message in one well-known Welsh rhyme:

> *There is great weeping and shouting*
> *In Ystrad-ffin this year;*
> *And the hewn stones melt into lead*
> *In fear of Twm Siôn Cati.*

The majority of the tales and anecdotes, however, portray him as a Welsh equivalent of Robin

Hood – a popular hero who robbed from the rich and gave to the poor.

Once he met a very poor man who wanted to buy a cauldron. 'Come with me', said Twm, 'and I'll get you one for free.' They both went into a shop and Twm told the shopkeeper that there was a hole in one of his cauldrons. The shopkeeper was furious. 'Place the pot over your head', said Twm, 'and you will see the hole.' This he did, but while he searched for the hole in the dark, Twm and the poor man left the shop with a brand new pot!

Another story tells how Twm, angered by the wickedness and cruelty of a fellow highwayman, decided to teach him a lesson. He disguised himself as a poor farmer and rode a tired, skinny old horse, its saddle-bags full of shells, to a place where the robber used to lurk in ambush. The cruel highwayman sprang from the bushes and held him at gunpoint. Twm pretended to be terrified, but instead of meekly handing over his money he threw the bags over the hedge. The highwayman scrambled after them. Twm then leapt from his own horse onto the robber's beautiful mare, whose saddle-bags were already packed with stolen money, and galloped away.

Twm Siôn Cati's Cave and reputed hide-out is about a mile west of Ystrad-ffin.

37 TREGARON

38

Llanddewibrefi, Ceredigion

Llanddewibrefi, a village in the former county of Cardigan, is associated with mythological animals known as *Yr Ychen Bannog*, 'the long-horned oxen', which feature frequently in Welsh folklore. The legends always emphasize the oxen's great strength and size. An unlocated lake known as Llyn Llion, which once submerged the whole of Britain, never overflowed again because Hu Gadarn ('Hu the mighty'), with the assistance of the *Ychen Bannog*, succeeded in dragging the *afanc*, a water monster, out of the lake. There was a water monster, too, at Llyn yr Afanc, a pool on the River Conwy, near Betws-y-coed. Although a young girl enticed the *afanc* out of the water, it escaped to its old refuge with one of the girl's breasts in its claws. It was then left to the two *Ychen Bannog* to haul the chained *afanc* out of its hiding place. Such was the struggle that the eye of one of the oxen fell to the ground. It was so large that it formed a pool known ever since as Pwll Llygad Ych ('the pool of the ox's eye').

The legends also emphasize that there are only two of the *Ychen Bannog* in the whole country. They are lonely survivors and must never be separated. In the Mabinogion tale of Culhwch and Olwen the two *Ychen Bannog* (Nynniaw and Peibiaw) are separated by a mountain called Mynydd Banawg, and one of the tasks young Culhwch must fulfil before he can marry Olwen is to reunite the two oxen.

One legend describes how the two oxen, while pulling an enormous stone to build the Church of Llanddewibrefi, opened a long furrow (*cwys*) on the mountain known to this day as Cwys yr Ychen Bannog. (It is three miles north of Tregaron and is now used as a public footpath.) One of the oxen died in the effort. Its partner, before he too died, bellowed nine times and split open a huge rock which was an obstacle to the passage of the stone. A local Welsh rhyme emphasizes the onomastic element in the legend (*brefu*(i) = to bellow):

Speckled Llanddewibrefi
Where the ox bellowed nine times
Until it split open the Foelallt Rock.

A horn-core known as *Mabcorn yr Ych Bannog,* now to be seen at the Welsh Folk Museum, was preserved for centuries at Llanddewibrefi Church. It belonged to the great urus *Bos primogenius,* the wild, long-horned cattle which existed in Britain in pre-Roman times. Thus, the Welsh *Ychen Bannog* legends have a substratum of tradition underlying them which dates back to an age before the great long-horned urus became extinct in Wales. The white 'wild' cattle, associated with such estates in Wales as Dinefwr and Glynllifon, are believed to be the *Ychen Bannog's* remote descendants. (See also item 44.)

39

Nantmel, Radnorshire

Nantmel is a village situated between Rhaeadr and Llandrindod Wells, in the former county of Radnor. About two miles south of the village lies a lake called Llyn Gwyn, which folk tradition associates with Gwyn ap Nudd, King of the Fairies and Lord of the Underworld. He had power to carry people through the sky, and in certain legends he even challenges the supremacy of saints. He is also portrayed as the one who leads his Underworld Dogs, *Cŵn Annwfn*, to seek out the lost souls of the dead.

Another tradition relates how this lake was once used by the monks of Strata Florida to supply the abbey with fish. When the abbey was destroyed in 1539 by Henry VIII's soldiers a monk prayed that every trout caught thereafter in the lake should testify to the wrong which had been done. From that time onwards, it is said, each trout caught made a croaking noise, and people refused to eat the fish. (See item 36.)

40

Maesyfed (New Radnor), Radnorshire

Dr John Lloyd, 'Silver John' (*c.* 1740–1814?), was a bone specialist and a member of the Lloyd family, well known in the counties of Radnor and Hereford for its interest in divination and medicine.

It is believed that 'Silver John', so called because of the silver buttons on his coat, was murdered by the men of New Radnor who wanted to steal the buttons and other pieces of silver on his clothes which he had received as payment for his services. His body was discovered beneath the frozen waters of Llyn Hilyn, near New Radnor, in the 'Year of the Great Frost' (1814?). The lake was thereafter troubled with his spirit. His grave is on the slopes of Radnor Forest and it was once believed that the grass on his grave would always be green.

Silver John's death is commemorated in a verse which used to incense the people of New Radnor whenever they heard it being sung:

> *'Silver John is dead and gone' –*
> *So they came home a-singing;*
> *The Radnor Boys pulled out his eyes*
> *And set the bells a-ringing.*

41 GLASGWM

41

Glasgwm, Radnorshire

In former times there was a beautiful small bell, called Bangu, in Glasgwm Church, which was reputedly the gift of Saint David and had been brought there by magic oxen.

Objects associated with saints were regarded as sacred relics, and were afforded great respect. It was also believed that such objects had supernatural powers, and if anyone dared treat them with irreverence, God's vengeance would fall upon those responsible. Thus was the wonderful Bangu bell regarded.

Once a woman took the bell to the nearby town of Rhaeadr. Her husband was imprisoned in the castle and she believed that if she rang the bell he would be released. But the guards seized it and chased the woman out of town. That night the town of Rhaeadr was utterly destroyed by fire. The only part of it which escaped the flames was the wall on which the sacred Bangu bell was hanging.

The above legend was recorded by Giraldus Cambrensis in his book *Descriptio Kambriae* ('Description of Wales', 1193). Giraldus (*c.* 1146–1223), also known as Gerallt Gymro and Gerald de Barry, was one of the greatest medieval writers from Wales, and in his two interesting and important books, *Itinerarium Kambriae* ('An Account of the Journey through Wales', 1191) and *Descriptio Kambriae*, he gave a valuable and vivid description of the folklore of Wales in his day and age.

42

Cilmeri, Sir Frycheiniog

On the banks of the River Irfon at Cilmeri near Builth Wells, a stone monument was raised in 1956 to commemorate Llywelyn ap Gruffudd, 'Llywelyn our Last Prince' (*c*. 1225–82). On 11 December 1282, after he had unsuccessfully defended Irfon Bridge at Cilmeri against the might of Edward I's army, Llywelyn was returning almost alone to rejoin his own soldiers on land above the river when an English knight, Stephen de Francton, probably ignorant of the Prince's identity, pierced his body with a spear. Later Edward arranged for Llywelyn's severed head to be crowned with ivy and carried on a pole through the streets of London to the sound of horns and trumpets and great merriment. His body, it is believed, was buried at Cwm-hir Abbey, near Rhaeadr.

With the death of Llywelyn, 'the candle of kings', Wales lost her independence. To his own people it was no less than a national catastrophe, and the anguish and grief is clearly felt in Gruffydd ab yr Ynad Coch's renowned elegy (translation):

> *Do you not see the rush of wind and rain?*
> *Do you not see the oak-trees crashing together?*
> *Do you not see the ocean scourging the shore?*
> *Do you not see the truth is portending?*
> *Do you not see the sun hurtling through the sky?*
> *Do you not see the stars have fallen?*
> *Have you no belief in God, foolish men?*
> *Do you not see the world is ending? …*
> *Head of fair Llywelyn, sharp the world's fear,*

An iron spike through it.
Head of my lord, harsh pain is mine;
Head of my spirit left speechless.
Head that had honour in nine hundred lands;
Nine hundred feasts for him.
Head of a king …

Near Aberedw there is a cave known as Ogof Llywelyn. Legend claims that the Prince came here to hide shortly before he was killed. When he left the cave he asked a local blacksmith, called Madog Goch, to re-fix the shoes of his horse, back to front, to deceive the enemy. This he did, and Llywelyn journeyed through the snow towards Builth. But the Normans came and tortured Madog Goch until he confessed and told them where Llywelyn had gone. Although there is probably no truth in this legend, the inhabitants of Aberedw were thereafter nicknamed *'Bradwyr Aberedw'* ('the traitors of Aberedw').

Tradition also tells us that the land in Cilmeri where Llywelyn died was once full of broom, but since that fateful day it has never grown in that vale, because it still mourns the death of 'Our Last Prince'.

43

Llyn Syfaddan(Llan-gors Lake), Brecknockshire

Two folk legends are associated with Llyn Syfaddan, Llan-gors Lake, Brecknockshire. One is based on the international theme of the palace or town that is drowned because of the wickedness of its ruler. (See also item 21.) The land beneath the lake once belonged to a cruel and greedy princess. Her lover was poor but she agreed to marry him on condition that he brought her much wealth – she did not care how. So he robbed and murdered a wealthy merchant. But the merchant's ghost returned to warn the couple that their crime would be avenged upon the ninth generation of their family. They ignored the warning, however, and exulted in their wealth and evil ways. They lived so remarkably long that they saw their descendants of the ninth generation. But one evening during a great feast of celebration for the whole family, a terrible flood burst from the hills and drowned the land and all its inhabitants.

The second legend is based on the tradition (recorded by Giraldus Cambrensis) that *Adar Syfaddan* ('the birds of Syfaddan') which lived on the lake would sing on the command of the true prince of South Wales, and none other. Sometime during the reign of Henry I, when the English had captured almost the whole of Brecknock, it is said that Gruffudd ap Rhys, Prince of South Wales (*d.* 1136), was one day walking along the banks of the lake in the company of two Norman lords. The birds refused to sing at their command, but at the command of Gruffudd ap Rhys they sang loudly to proclaim him the true Prince.

44

Llyn y Fan Fach, Carmarthenshire

Llyn y Fan Fach is a mountain lake, near Llanddeusant, and associated with one of the most famous Welsh folk tales. According to the legend the son of Blaen Sawdde farm, Myddfai, fell in love with a beautiful lady from the lake. After offering her three kinds of bread (dry, moist and slightly baked) she promised to marry him, but on one condition: he should not give her 'three blows without a cause'. Her father gave her as dowry from the lake the best stock of cattle, sheep, goats and horses in the country. They lived happily for many years at a farm called Esgair Llaethdy and had three sons, but she was struck lightly and thoughtlessly by her husband on three occasions: when she was reluctant to attend a baptism service in the neighbourhood; when she cried at a wedding; and when she laughed at a funeral service. After the third blow she returned to the lake calling on all her cattle and animals to follow her (translation):

> *Hump-brindled, Hornless-brindled,*
> *Rump-brindled, White-freckled …*
> *With the white bull from the King's court,*
> *And the little black calf which is on the hook,*
> *You too return home, fully recovered.*
> (Note the 'little black calf' in the illustration.)

The mother reappeared on several occasions to her three sons at places called Pant y Meddygon ('the physicians' hollow') and Llidiart y Meddygon ('the physicians' gate') and taught them the virtues of plants and herbs. Rhiwallon, the eldest son, and his three sons became physicians to Rhys Gryg, Lord of Dinefwr (*d.* 1234), and founded a long line of famous physicians

known as the *'Physicians of Myddfai'*. Their folk remedies were recorded in manuscripts, the earliest dating from the thirteenth century. Years later the text was published in a book, The Physicians of Myddvai, edited by John Williams and translated by John Pughe (1861).

The Llyn y Fan Fach legend is based on folk memory of a people who lived in primitive homes and caves on the shores of lakes. It is believed that the description of the cattle is consistent with the type of cattle which were in Britain between the Iron Age and the Dark Ages. The early legend of the 'Lady of the Lake' was possibly linked with the much later tradition of the Myddfai Physicians and Rhys Gryg when 'the white bull from the King's court' (descendants of the early urus) came to be identified with the white cattle of the royal court of Dinefwr. (See also item 38.)

Later the lake became associated with a number of beliefs and traditions. It was believed, for example, that there were seven echoes between the banks of Tyle Gwyn and Gwter Goch; that there was an unnatural suction in the surrounding rocks; and that the lake was bottomless. It was also a popular custom in the nineteenth century for people to visit the lake on the first Sunday in August each year to observe the waters 'boiling' – a sure sign that the 'lady of the lake' was about to appear. Indeed, some people to this day believe that the 'lovely maidens of Myddfai' (mentioned in a local rhyme) are remote descendants of the beautiful 'lady of the lake'.

45

Nanhyfer (Nevern), Pembrokeshire

A remarkable group of antiquities and traditions is connected with Saint Brynach's Church at Nevern. A few yards from the church a path leads to a small cross, known as *Croes y Pererinion*, the Pilgrims' Cross, carved in the rock. The path was used by saints and pilgrims on their journey to St. David's.

In the churchyard stands Saint Brynach's Cross, regarded as one of the three finest Celtic crosses in Wales. According to tradition, it is from this cross on 7 April (Saint Brynach's Day) that the cuckoo's song is first heard in Pembrokeshire. In the old days it used to be said that the priest was reluctant to commence the service on this day until he had heard the cuckoo's song. One year the bird was very late arriving and the congregation was patiently waiting. Eventually the cuckoo arrived, but it was so exhausted that after singing for a brief moment it died.

Saint Brynach (also known as Brynach Wyddel, 'Brynach the Irishman', being of Irish lineage) was probably born at Cemaes, Pembrokeshire. He went on a pilgrimage to Rome and spent some years in Brittany. But he returned to Wales and settled at Nevern, living as a hermit on the nearby hill of Carn Ingli, where, it is said, the angels administered to him. Hence the name of the hill is thought to be derived from *Mons Angelorum*, or Carn Angylion, 'the mount of angels'.

There is also in the churchyard at Nevern an ancient tree known as *Yr Ywen Waedlyd*, 'The Bleeding Yew'. A red exudation flows from its trunk. Popular folk tradition maintains that a man, possibly a monk, was hanged on this tree. Before dying he swore that the tree would bleed forever as evidence of his innocence.

46

Abergwaun (Fishguard), Pembrokeshire

A stone above the sea at Strumble Head (Pen-caer), near Fishguard, commemorates the landing of the French troops on 22 February 1797. This was the last foreign invasion of Britain. A French expeditionary force, commanded by an American officer named Tate, sailed up the Bristol Channel in the hope of starting a peasant rebellion in England against the landowners, but high winds forced them to land on the Welsh coast. The invaders set up their headquarters in the cellar of Tre Hywel farm, near Goodwick. Two days later Lord Cawdor advanced on the drunken French soldiers with the Castlemartin Yeomanry. They retreated to the beach below Goodwick where an inscribed stone now marks the spot where they surrendered on 24 February.

Local tradition maintains that the French soldiers surrendered because several women of the district, led by the formidable Jemima Nicholas, dressed in red cloaks and petticoats and boldly marched towards the French who mistook them for the British army. Jemima Nicholas became famous as the 'General of the Red Army'. It is said, for example, that she caught a number of the French with her pitchfork. She died in 1832 and is buried in St. Mary's Church, Fishguard, where there is a memorial to her.

Folk traditions concerning the 'landing of the French' are still alive in the Fishguard district. A clock at Bristgarn farm, for example, still has a bullet mark in its case, and on another farm, The Cots, they still tell the story of how the mother's life was saved when she lifted her day-old baby in her arms for a French soldier to see it.

47

Tyddewi (St David's), Pembrokeshire

From the Middle Ages until the present day St. David's has been an important place of pilgrimage, especially since David (Dewi) was officially recognised by Pope Callixtus as a saint in 1120 and later became universally acknowledged as the patron saint of Wales. It was here, where the Cathedral stands today, that David founded his church at Glyn Rhosyn (*Vallis Rosina*), and eventually became one of the most important leaders of the Celtic Church in Wales. Disciples flocked to him, in spite of his stern self-denial and the rigid discipline of his monastery, for he was noted for his gentle nature.

Like many other saints whose biographies were written centuries after they had died, David was credited with the working of innumerable miracles. The majority of these were first noted by Rhygyfarch in his *Vita Davidis* ('Life of David'), written in Latin towards the end of the eleventh century.

The name of David's father was Sant, son of Ceredig, King of Ceredigion (Cardigan). His mother's name was Non. At the time of his birth a great storm, we are told, raged across the Bay of Non in Pembrokeshire and all the surrounding country, but Non's little cottage was bathed in sunshine.

Legend claims that there was no water near his monastery. David prayed, and a well appeared at his feet. Many of the other wells associated with David, such as Ffynnon Feddyg ('the physician's well'), near Aberaeron, are said to have burst from the ground at places where he miraculously healed the blind, the lame and the sick. His old teacher, Paulinus, we are told, was blind, but David gave him back his sight. There are also miraculous objects and relics associated with the patron saint. For example, his wonderful *Bangu* bell. (See item 41.)

At a meeting of the Church Senate in Llanddewibrefi the assembled bishops could not make themselves heard above the noise of the crowd, but when David began to preach a mound suddenly rose beneath him and everyone could hear his sermon clearly. Following this Senate meeting David was proclaimed Archbishop. He died (according to Rhygyfarch) on 1 March 589, and a host of angels took his soul to heaven in glory and honour.

In 1398 Archbishop Arundel ordered the church to celebrate Saint David's Day on the first of March each year, and since the eighteenth century in particular, this day has been regarded in Wales as a national festival. As early as the sixteenth century (during the reign of Mary Tudor) the leek was worn by Welshmen on 1 March and has since been adopted as a national emblem. One legend relates how the Welsh were once fighting the pagan English in a field full of leeks. Saint David ordered the Welshmen to wear leeks on their helmets to help them identify themselves. But a more likely reason for associating the leek with Saint David and eventually adopting it as a national emblem is because it was once regarded as an essential ingredient in the diet of the Welsh saints and the Welsh people in general, especially during Lent. It had also valuable medicinal virtues; it was widely used in divination; and, most importantly, it was a symbol of purity and immortality

48

Casnewy-Bach (Little Newcastle), Pembrokeshire

Little Newcastle, between Haverfordwest and Fishguard, was the birthplace of one of the most famous Welsh sea-pirates, Bartholomew Roberts, 'Barti Ddu', or 'Black Bart' (1682?–1722). He went to sea at an early age, but unlike Henry Morgan (1635?–88), the renowned pirate from Gwent, Bartholomew Roberts was a pirate for only the last five years of his life. In 1718 he was second mate on a merchant ship, 'The Princess', sailing to West Africa, when he and his crew were captured by pirates. They were all forced to join the new ship and live as pirates under the command of another Welshman, Captain Hywel Davies (Hywel Dafydd). In a few weeks Hywel Dafydd was killed and Black Bart was chosen to succeed him as captain.

Shortly afterwards they took a ship heavily laden with gold and silver, tobacco, sugar and skins, but while Barti Ddu was busy selling the merchandise on land and spending the money, one of his crew escaped and sailed away with his ship. Barti found another, smaller ship and sailed to one of the ports of Newfoundland. There, it is said, he sank all the ships in the harbour except one, which he took and sailed to the coast of Guinea. He won great fame as a pirate in the Caribbean, and legends are told of his many adventures. He was described as a tall, dignified man of unusual bravery.

Early one morning in February 1722 his ship, 'The Royal fortune', was attacked without warning by the British Royal Marines, near Cape Lopez. Barti Ddu was shot in the throat and thrown over-board into the sea in his resplendent dress. And that is how the adventurous life of the Welsh sea-pirate ended:

Barti Ddu from Casnewy-bach,
The tall seaman with a hearty laugh.

(Quoted from the Welsh ballad by the poet I. D. Hooson.)

49

Yr Efail Wen, Pembrokeshire

The numerous toll-gates in South Wales during the first half of the nineteenth century imposed an additional financial burden on the already poverty-stricken agricultural community. At last the people took the law into their own hands and it was only after the Rebecca Rioters had destroyed many of the gates that the injustice was removed. Groups of men, often with blackened faces and wearing women's clothes, attacked the gates, usually by night. The Efail Wen toll-gate (on the road from Crymych to Clunderwen and near the villages of Mynachlog-ddu and Llangolman on the border between Pembrokeshire and Carmarthenshire) was the first gate to be destroyed on 13 May 1839.

Many tales are told of the activities of the rioters, 'The Daughters of Rebecca' as they were called. Urging them on was the daring 'Rebecca' herself, a man dressed as a woman. In some districts Rebecca wore a white gown with horse-hair wig. Elsewhere she appeared as an old, blind woman carrying a staff, and before destroying a gate she would perform a little ceremony opening with these words: 'My children, something is in my way, I cannot go on.' The 'Rebecca' who led the attack on the Efail Wen toll-gate was the gigantic Thomas Rees of Carnabwth, 'Twm Carnabwth', Mynachlog-ddu. It is said that he was unable to get suitable clothes until he borrowed those of 'Beca Fawr' ('Big Beca') from Llangolman, and that is why he was addressed as 'Beca' and the name 'the Rebecca Riots' came into use. A more likely reason for the use of the term 'Rebecca', however, is that it was inspired by a reference in the Book of Genesis, XXIV, 60: 'And they blessed Rebekah and said unto her, Our sister, be thou the mother of thousands of ten thousands, and let thy seed possess the gate of those which hate them.'

Before the end of 1843 toll-gates had been destroyed in all three counties of West Wales and also in Glamorgan, Brecknock and Radnor. Soon afterwards, however, as a result of a Government Commission, Road Boards were established to re-assess the whole problem, and the number of toll-gates was greatly reduced.

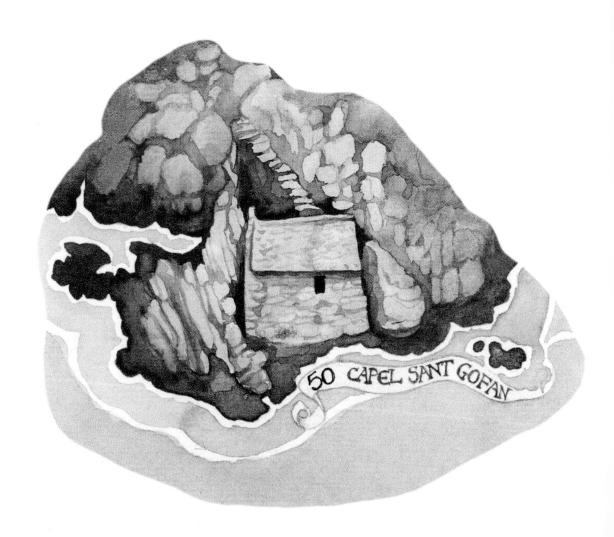

50 CAPEL SANT GOFAN

50

Capel Sant Gofan (St. Govan's Chapel), Pembrokeshire

Perched in a ravine in the cliffs overlooking the sea at St. Govan's Head, Pembrokeshire, is the tiny Saint Govan's Chapel. A long flight of steps cut into the rock leads down to this ancient and unique building, and it is a popular belief that the number of steps varies, depending on whether the person counting them is climbing up or down.

The altar and seats in the chapel are of stone. In the east wall a doorway leads into a vertical cleft in the rock. This cavity is in the form of a man's body, and it is said that when Govan fled from his pagan persecutors the rock miraculously opened to let him in and then closed again to conceal him from his enemies. When they were gone, it re-opened. It has long been regarded as a wishing cell. A wish made while standing in the cleft and facing the wall will be granted, provided you do not change your mind before turning round. One legend claims that Christ himself was once hiding in the vertical cleft and that the marks of his body may be seen there to this day. He fled to the chapel when persecuted by his Jewish enemies.

It is said that Saint Govan's bell once hung above the chapel's roof and that it would sometimes ring on its own accord. Saint Govan's healing well is situated just below the chapel, while for centuries the red clay in the surrounding cliffs has been credited with the power of healing sore eyes.

According to one tradition, Saint Govan was a disciple of Saint David. Another tradition maintains that he was a thief who fled to this area for safety and who, in gratitude for the miraculous hiding place, became a convert and built the chapel in praise of God. One romantic version says that Saint Govan was Sir Gawain, one of King Arthur's knights who, after the death of Arthur, came here to spend the rest of his life as a hermit. This tradition is probably explained by the similarity between Govan and Gawain, or its French form Gauvain (in Welsh Gwalchmai).

51

Caerfyrddin (Carmarthen)

The Roman name for the old fort in Carmarthen was *moridunum*, 'the sea fort'. The Welsh eventually renamed it Caerfyrddin (*caer* = fort), assuming that Myrddin was a person's name rather than a natural derivation from the Latin. Thus, the legend of Myrddin (Merlin), the wizard, so widespread in the Celtic countries and on the Continent, became associated with Caerfyrddin, 'Myrddin's fort'.

In the Welsh version of the legend, founded upon the primitive theme of the 'Wild Man in the Woods', Myrddin, after his defeat at the Battle of Arfderydd (the modern Arthuret, near Carlisle) in 573, lost his reason and fled to Coed Celyddon, the Caledonian Forest in the then Welsh-speaking Scottish Lowlands. While wandering in misery for half a century with only a piglet and other wild animals to keep him company, he became a prophet. From the ninth century onwards his prophecies were contained in poems claimed to have been composed by Myrddin himself, many of which are included in *Llyfr Du Caerfyrddin* (The Black Book of Carmarthen), written about 1250.

Most of the more recent Welsh traditions about Myrddin are centred around Caerfyrddin. Stones in the district are connected with his prophecies, and his famous oak tree in the centre of the town was for many years carefully safeguarded by the municipal authorities. Its stump is now on display at the County Museum, although one or two of the town's inhabitants may still be rather apprehensive about its removal and might quote Merlin's old prophecy:

> *When Merlin's tree shall tumble down,*
> *Then shall fall Carmarthen town.*

According to one tradition the great magician is still alive in a cave in Bryn Myrddin ('Merlin's Hill', near Abergwili, about two miles from the town), kept in bonds of enchantment for ever by a woman he once loved. At certain times of the year it is said that people used to hear his groans bewailing his folly in revealing to a woman the secrets of his magic. Another tradition maintains that Merlin has a smithy inside this hill and that the sound of the blacksmiths may still be heard if one kneels to the ground and listens carefully.

52 CYDWELI

52

Cydweli, Pembrokeshire

Cydweli (Kidwelly) Castle is associated with one of the heroines of Welsh history, Gwenllian, daughter of Gruffudd ap Cynan, King of Gwynedd, and the wife of Gruffydd ap Rhys Tewdwr, the last King of the Deheubarth (South West Wales). Following the death of Henry I in 1135 the lords of South Wales rebelled against the Normans who had occupied their territories. But while Gruffydd ap Rhys was away in Gwynedd seeking the support of Gwenllian's father, the Norman knight Maurice de Londres attacked Gruffydd's lands. In her husband's absence Gwenllian led an army of Deheubarth men against the Norman fortress of Cydweli and Maurice de Londres's soldiers. But she was killed outside the castle on Mynydd y Garreg at a place known to this day as *Maes Gwenllian* ('Gwenllian's field'). Her son, Morgan, was also killed, and her other son, Maelgwn, was taken prisoner.

For centuries afterwards the place where Gwenllian died was troubled by the ghost of a headless woman. One moonlit night a local man ventured in the name of God and Christ to ask the woman why she was wandering in such a manner. 'Alas', she answered, 'I cannot rest until I find my head, please help me.' For three nights the man searched the area and eventually found it and returned it. Gwenllian's ghost was never seen again wandering on Mynydd y Garreg and the slopes of Cydweli Castle.

53

Tre Rheinallt (Reynoldston), Glanorganshire

On Cefn Bryn Common, near Reynoldston, in the Gower Peninsula, lies a huge stone known as *Coeten Arthur* ('Arthur's quoit').

No other historical character has figured so prominently in Welsh folklore as King Arthur, the military leader of the Britons who lived at the end of the fifth century and the beginning of the sixth century. By the seventh and eighth centuries he had become to be considered a supreme warrior, the *dux bellorum* (the commander in battle), as Nennius(?) describes him in his *Historia Brittonum* (*c.* 800). He was the champion defender of the Britons against the attacks of the Angles and Saxons from the Continent, especially in East and South East Britain. Later, more and more fabulous feats were attributed to him, and these, undoubtedly, formed an essential part of the repertoire of Welsh storytellers in the Middle Ages, and have done so ever since.

Huge stones have for centuries aroused man's curiosity, and imaginative stories have been told to explain them. Some stones were said to have been carried by giants and giantesses or thrown from an enormous distance. One such giant was the mighty King Arthur, and stones associated with him were often called *Coeten* or *Coetan Arthur*. The large stone of Cefn Bryn Common was merely a 'pebble in his boot'. Arthur was on his way to the Battle of Camlan when he felt the 'pebble' hurting him, and he then threw the stone a distance of over seven miles. (At Camlan he was mortally wounded. The date of the battle, according to the chronicle *Annales Cambriae*, was 537.)

Until the end of the nineteenth century young local girls used to meet at midnight around this stone when the moon was full. A cake made of barley-meal and honey and wetted with milk was placed on the stone. Then, to test the fidelity of their lovers, the girls crawled on their hands and knees three times around the stone. If their lovers were faithful, it was believed that they would soon join them.

53 TRE RHEINALLT

54

CASTELL PENNARD

54

Castell Pennard (Pennard Castle), Glamorganshire

Pennard Castle, once the fortress of Rhys ap Iestyn, today lies in ruins among sand dunes on the Gower Peninsula. According to legend, a prince of North Wales gave his daughter in marriage to Rhys for his valour in battle. On the wedding night, at the height of the celebrations, the sound of sweet music was heard outside the castle walls. In the moonlight a host of fairies were seen dancing on the grass near the castle gatehouse. The inebriated Prince Rhys ordered his men to drive the little folk away, but his wife was astonished at his cruel behaviour and warned him that a terrible misfortune would occur if they were not allowed to stay. Her lord, however, replied arrogantly that he feared no one of this world or any other. Followed by the bravest of his men he went out to battle with the fairies, but the little people faded before them, like the morning mist, and not one of them was touched.

Suddenly a warning voice rang out: 'Thou hast wantonly spoilt our innocent sport, proud chief. Thy lofty castle and proud town shall be no more.' And at once a terrible sandstorm blew up, burying the castle, the town and all its inhabitants.

This legend is probably based on folk memory of the castle's constant battle against the encroaching sand dunes that finally engulfed it in the sixteenth century. Indeed, during the 300 years that the castle was occupied this was the only real battle it ever fought.

55

Ogof Craig y Dinas (Craig y Dinas Cave), Glamorganshire

A Welsh drover with a hazelwood staff in his hand once met a wizard on London Bridge. The wizard asked the Welshman to lead him to the tree from which the hazelwood staff had been cut. This he did and at the base of the tree they found a hidden passage leading to a cave, known today as Ogof Craig y Dinas, near Pontneddfechan, in the Vale of Neath.

At the entrance to the cave there was a large bell and inside the cave they saw King Arthur and his warriors sleeping beside two heaps of gold and silver. The wizard told the Welshman that he could take away as much gold and silver as he wanted, but he warned him never to touch the bell. If he accidentally did so, one of the warriors would awake and ask: 'Is it day?', in which case he should reply: 'No, sleep on.' Twice the Welshman became too greedy, overloaded himself and touched the bell accidentally, but each time he remembered to give the correct answer. On the third occasion, however, he failed to reply and he was beaten so badly by the warriors that he was crippled for life, and never again could he or any of his friends find the entrance to the cave.

This is one version of a popular legend based on the international theme of the 'vanished undying hero'. In times of distress, in particular, Welsh poets and storytellers from the ninth to the fifteenth centuries would endeavour to raise the spirit and patriotic zeal of their countrymen by forecasting a great revival and the coming of the long-awaited *Mab Darogan*, 'the prophesied son', who would lead his people once again to victory. The great deliverer was one of the remarkable heroes of the past: Cynan, Cadwaladr or Owain. People came to believe that such super-warriors were not dead but asleep in some cave, awaiting the day to be recalled to battle. In more recent Welsh folk traditions the sleeping hero is usually King Arthur. There are caves associated with Arthur in Snowdonia, Llanllyfni and Llanuwchllyn, Gwynedd; Caerleon, Gwent; Vale of Tywi, Dyfed; and Llantrisant, Ystradyfodwg and Pontneddfechan, Glamorgan. Some of these caves, especially those in South Wales, are known by the name 'Craig y Dinas'; others are simply called 'Ogof Arthur' or 'Arthur's Cave'.

In some versions, relating to caves in Glamorgan in particular, the Sleeping Hero is Owain Glyndŵr (*c.* 1354–*c.* 1416). In other versions the hero is Owain ap Thomas ap Rhodri ('Owain Lawgoch' or 'Yvain de Galles', *c.* 1300–78), for example, caves at Troed-yr-aur and Llandybïe, Dyfed.

56

Llangynwyd, Glamorganshire

The old mansion of Cefn Ydfa, now in ruins, is situated in the parish of Llangynwyd, Tir Iarll, near Maesteg. This was the home of Ann Thomas (1704–27), 'The Maid of Cefn Ydfa', whose romantic and sad story is well known. Ann's true love was Wil Hopcyn, a local slater, plasterer and poet, but she was forced by her parents against her will to marry a wealthy solicitor, Anthony Maddocks. Wil, grieving, left the district, but later returned in response to Ann's earnest entreaty when she became mortally ill. She died in his arms, brokenhearted, at twenty three years of age. The beautiful song 'Bugeilio'r Gwenith Gwyn' (lit. 'shepherding the white wheat') is said to have been written by Wil Hopcyn to express his love for Ann. Ann Maddocks was buried in Llangynwyd churchyard and there, too, lies the body of Wil Hopcyn who died in 1741 at the age of 47.

Additional stories and anecdotes were added to the romance of Ann and Wil Hopcyn by Isaac Craigfryn Hughes in his novel *The Maid of Cefn Ydfa* (1881). Historians, however, doubt whether there is any historical basis to the Llangynwyd legend. Although a poet of the name Wil Hopcyn lived in the district, there is no definite proof that he was Ann Thomas's lover or that he composed the song. And yet, the tragic romance of 'The Maid of Cefn Ydfa' and Wil Hopcyn is still popular in Llangynwyd and throughout Wales.

57

Llanwynno, Glamorganshire

The most remarkable Welsh runner of all time, according to legend, was Griffith Morgan, better known as 'Guto Nyth Brân' (1700–37). He was born at Llwyn Celyn, near Hafod, Pontypridd, but moved shortly afterwards with his parents to a nearby smallholding called Nyth Brân in the parish of Llanwynno.

Numerous tales are told about Guto's astonishing feats as a runner. When he was a young lad no one in the district could keep pace with him, and he could easily catch the sheep on the mountain. At times his mother used to send him to Aberdare early in the morning to buy yeast. He would leave the house when his mother was putting the kettle on the fire in preparation for breakfast, and would return by the time the kettle had boiled! He was once sent by his father to the mountain to gather sheep and he brought them all down in a very short time without the assistance of a single dog. When he returned his father asked him whether he had any difficulty. 'No', he replied, 'the only trouble I had was with one old brown sheep. But when I finally caught it, I realized I had been chasing a hare!' When Guto went foxhunting, it is said that he always ran with the hounds. He often slept on a dung-heap in the belief that this would strengthen his legs.

Many a race he had won. Indeed, no one had ever beaten him. One story claims that he ran a race against the speedy horse of a country gentleman from Cardiganshire and won. But his most famous race of all was his last one. An Englishman, called Prince, challenged him to run twelve miles, for a great sum of money, from Newport, Gwent, to Bedwas Church, near Caerffili. It is said that Guto stopped on his way to talk to supporters, but although his opponents had placed broken glass on his path, he ran the whole distance in fifty three minutes and won the race. 'Siân o'r Siop' was his greatest admirer, and in exultation she rushed towards Guto and slapped him on the back. Seconds later he died of heart failure.

'Guto Nyth Brân' was buried in Llanwynno Church and a heart was later engraved on his gravestone to remind people of the cause of his death. Ballads in memory of Guto were composed by the poets I. D. Hooson and Harri Webb.

58

Gilfach Fargoed, Glamorganshire

In days gone by no district in Wales had more fairies than the Rhymney Valley. And nowhere were they more happy. On moonlit nights they would dance and sing merrily. But then a cruel giant came to live in Gilfach Fargoed. His home was a high tower with a garden surrounding it. The fairies' song was heard no more and no longer were they seen dancing. They were forced to hide in fear day and night. The giant had a huge cudgel with a poisonous snake twisted around it, and he would kill and eat any fairy he caught.

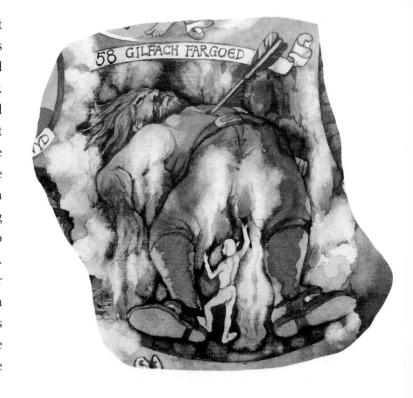

One young lad had lost both his mother and father, and he thought long for a way to kill the giant. Eventually he decided on a plan and told it to the Queen of the Fairies. Because he was a fairy himself he knew the language of birds, and one night he went to see the owl who lived in an oak-tree at Pencoed Fawr, Bedwellte to ask for her assistance. And this was his plan. The giant used to meet under a large apple-tree outside his home almost every night to court a witch. Other birds, although greatly fearing the giant, were to help the owl fix a bow and arrow on the apple-tree, and then the owl was to shoot the giant. One night the giant was waiting in his usual place, but the witch was late and the giant fell asleep. While he was sleeping the owl shot the arrow and killed the giant, then flew back to Pencoed Fawr, singing with joy.

In a short while the witch arrived. The birds were no longer afraid. They attacked her from all directions and killed her. Before dying, however, she swore that henceforth all apples growing on trees outside the garden walls would be sour. And that is why, according to the legend, the fruit of wild apple trees is sour.

Following the death of the giant and the witch, the snake eventually died of fear. The young lad buried it and planted flowers on the grave which ever since have been known as *Blodau'r Neidr*, 'Snake Flowers' (*Silene dioca*).

The giant had plenty of gold and silver in his home and the queen distributed it among the fairies. About a dozen of them went to farm near the giant's home, but they could not stay long there because his body was stinking. They dug a huge pit to bury him, but still could not endure the smell. One of the fairies suggested burning the body, and this they did, but the whole pit went on fire, and they had to carry much water to extinguish it. Then they saw that the sides of the pit were of black crystal stone. They carried some of it to their homes and set it alight. It proved to be an excellent means of heating. And that is how, according to the legend, coal was first discovered in the Rhymney Valley.

After the death of the giant and the witch the owl used to come every moonlit night from Pencoed Fawr to Gilfach Fargoed to celebrate, and her descendants are there to this day continuing their song of joy, because their friends, the fairies, may once again sing and dance in the Rhymney Valley.

59

Castell Ogwr (Ogmore Castle), Glamorganshire

A familiar ghost known as *Y Ladi Wen* ('the white lady') once guarded the treasure in Ogmore Castle. One night a brave man ventured towards the *Ladi Wen*. She led him to the castle tower and ordered him to lift a heavy stone in its floor. There the man found a cauldron full of gold pieces. 'You may take half of them,' said the ghost, 'but leave the other half to me.' This he did and replaced the stone.

A few days later the man was tempted to seek the rest of the treasure. He went to the castle tower and filled his pockets with gold. When he was just about to return, he was met by the 'white Lady'. She accused him of stealing and attacked him. This time she had sharp claws and the man was badly hurt. He arrived home, but became very ill soon afterwards. Before he died he confessed his greed, and his friends called his illness 'the *Ladi Wen*'s revenge'.

There was an old belief that a person who died without disclosing hidden treasure could not rest in peace and that the person's ghost would return to torment the living and to seek assistance in returning the treasure to its rightful owner or to throw it downstream into a river. If it was thrown upstream the spirit still could not rest. There are a number of legends of ghosts seen near Ogmore Castle and the River Ogmore – some of them said to be searching for their hidden treasure.

Barbara, the wife of a tailor from Llantwit Major, was once a healthy happy person, until she began to be tormented by her mother-in-law's ghost. Before she died the old lady had given Barbara a bag full of money to share between members of the family. For many years, however, the tailor's wife did not disclose to anyone that she had the money. Finally, she agreed to fulfil the wishes of her mother-in-law's spirit. The money was to be thrown downstream into the River Ogmore. In her fear and confusion Barbara threw the money upstream, and because of this she and her family were still troubled by the ghost for many more years.

59 CASTELL OGWR

60

Pen-marc (Penmark), Glamorganshire

Among the numerous and very entertaining tales which endeavour to explain the meaning of Welsh Place-names (onomastic tales), many of them are associated with animals (for example, the *Ychen Bannog* and the *Afanc*, item 38). Another interesting example is the following tale referring to two names in Cardigan and South Glamorgan.

One of the Princes of North Wales had a remarkable horse, the strongest and swiftest in the kingdom. This horse was often used to carry urgent and important messages to King Arthur in his court in Somerset. On one occasion the horse galloped so fast that it fell dead in a place called to this day Cefn-march ('horse's ridge'), on a meadow at Gilfachreda, near Cei Newydd, Ceredigion. But its head travelled on until it fell, and the place where it fell became known as Pen-march ('horse's head'), which was later Anglicised to Penmark, now a village in the Vale of Glamorgan.

According to another tradition, not so well known, the name Pen-march is associated with March ap Meirchion, the king who had horse's ears. (See item 8.)

60 PEN-MARC

61 CASTELL COCH

61

Castell Coch, Glamorganshire

Castell Coch towers high on a woody hill above the village of Tongwynlais, and near the main road (A470) from Cardiff to Pontypridd and Merthyr Tudful. It was built in 1872, to a design by William Burges in Victorian Gothic style for the third Marquis of Bute, on the site of a castle built in the thirteenth century by Gilbert de Clare, Lord of Glamorgan.

On the same site there was an earlier castle owned by Ifor ap Cadifor, 'Ifor Bach' (*fl.* 1158), Lord of Senghennydd, Glamorgan. In 1158 he attacked Cardiff Castle and captured William, Earl of Gloucester, his wife and their son and refused to release them until William agreed to surrender to him all the lands which he had wrongfully occupied. Although very little is known about Ifor Bach, he was considered a leader of considerable courage. He once boasted that his twelve hundred men could defeat any twelve thousand of the enemy.

According to tradition Ifor Bach's treasure is kept in a deep vault in the castle at the opening of a tunnel leading to Cardiff Castle. The treasure is guarded day and night by three huge, ferocious eagles. At certain times of the year their unearthly screams terrorised the countryside and the noise of their flapping wings was like thunder. In the seventeenth and eighteenth centuries groups of armed men attempted to destroy the eagles, but without success. They were savagely attacked – even those whose arms had been blessed by a priest. No one will ever succeed in destroying the eagles, for they will stay in the castle to guard Ifor Bach's treasure until he returns with his 'twelve hundred men of Glamorgan'.

62

Casnewydd-ar-Wysg (Newport), Monmouthshire

Newport (Casnewydd-ar-Wysg, 'the new castle on the Usk') is situated in the old hundred of Gwynllwg (Wentlooge). It was once the home of Gwynllyw Filwr ('Gwynllyw, or Woolo, the soldier'). According to one testimony he was a very good man; according to another he was very wicked. His wife, Gwladus, was one of the reputed twenty four daughters of Brychan Brycheiniog, but she had been taken by force and he married her against her father's will. Near the Wye estuary there is a gorge called Pill Gwynllyw where Gwynllyw anchored his long boat. With this boat he used to attack ships and seamen and plunder their merchandise.

In vain did his wife Gwladus and their holy son, Cadog (Saint Cadog of Llancarfan) attempt to turn his mind to God. But one night he was told in a dream to go to a certain hill where he would find a white ox with a black star on its forehead. The next morning, to his great surprise, he saw the ox with a black star on its forehead on that very hill. He was struck with fear. Realizing that his dream was a message from God, from that day onwards he became a devout Christian. On the hill which he saw in his dream (now known as Stow Hill, in Newport) he built his church, and here today stands Saint Woolo's Cathedral.

It is said that disaster will befall anyone who desecrates this holy place. Once, when robbers cut into cheese which they had stolen from the church, it ran with blood. On another occasion when a band of pirates pillaged the church, their ship ran into a terrible storm. Saint Gwynllyw pursued them, riding on the wind, and recovered the church treasures.

62 CASNEWYDD-AR-WYSG

63

Rhisga (Risca), Monmouthshire

The people of Risca decided that they would like to have fine weather all the year round. They had noticed that it was always sunny when the cuckoo visited their town, thus concluding that the cuckoo was responsible for it. They planned, therefore, to keep the bird throughout the year and built high hedges all round the town. The cuckoo arrived, but when it was time to leave it just flew over the hedges, leaving the innocent people of Risca very angry with themselves that they had not built the hedges a little higher! And that is why the inhabitants of the town received the nickname 'The Cuckoos of Risca'.

This is an international folk tale, associated also, for example, with 'The Cuckoos of Dolwyddelan', Gwynedd, North Wales. In England the best known version relates to the 'Cuckoos of Pent'.

North of Risca is Twmbarlwm, a large hill fort, which has been the subject of many legends and traditions. On this hill a fierce battle was once fought between the wasps and the bees. When the wind was blowing from a certain direction, shepherds heard the sweet music of a 'mountain organ'. It was also believed that the Druids held their court of justice on Twmbarlwm hill. The bodies of guilty persons, it is said, were hurled into the valley below, known ever since as Dyffryn y Gladdfa ('the valley of the burial ground').

Welsh Folk Customs

There has always been a close relationship between folk customs and folk tales. The majority of folk customs and also folk tales (legends in particular) are based on folk beliefs. For example, it was believed that the Fairies feared iron and that an unbaptized baby was in danger of being snatched away by evil spirits and replaced by a peevish fairy offspring. These two beliefs lie at the heart of the custom of placing a poker or iron tongs across the cradle of an unbaptized baby as a protective charm.

There are accounts in Welsh tradition of parents who actually believed that their child had been replaced by an unearthly creature, a belief founded in the disease and fear characteristic of the age. With the passage of time many of these accounts of actual personal paranormal experiences became more and more stereotyped and schematic and were told as folk legends. Folk customs and folk tales were also closely linked on the social plane. Customs and festivities, pastimes and recreation often went hand in hand with storytelling.

In designing the accompanying illustrated map of Wales, therefore, although the main purpose was to present a selection of Welsh folk tales, it was decided to include an illustrated surround on the theme of folk customs. With one exception (love spoons) they all relate to calendar or seasonal customs. Those on the left are associated with the Christmas Season and the New Year: Hunting the Wren, *Calennig*, *Y Fari Lwyd*, and Wassailing. The customs on the right are associated with Love Spoons, May Dancing, and *Y Gaseg Fedi* (Harvest Mare). A brief description of these customs follows, based on Trefor M. Owen's *Welsh Folk Customs* (1959), from which the quotations are taken unless otherwise noted. Examples of the specimens associated with these customs are exhibited in the galleries of St Fagans National Museum of History.

Calennig

From very early times and in many parts of the world Christmastide and the New Year have been an occasion for celebration and rejoicing. After the winter solstice there was a shortening of the long winter nights and a 'heartening promise of the return of spring and summer, and of the rebirth of plant life.' It was also a time for the expression of good wishes for the coming year, this being the chief significance of the *calennig* (New Year's Gift) custom.

Early on New Year's Day groups of children would proceed from house to house until noon, carrying with them an apple or orange mounted on three short wooden skewers and decorated with oats (and sometimes raisins) and a sprig of evergreen, usually holly. The children sang or chanted verses and greetings wishing the families health and prosperity for the coming year. In return they would receive fruit or a few pennies – new pennies, if possible. By today the custom is observed only in a few areas and the children no longer carry the decorated apple or orange with them.

Y Fari Lwyd

The three customs known as *Y Fari Lwyd*, Wassailing and Hunting the Wren, the origins of which may be in a pre-Christian fertility cult, were celebrated throughout the Christmas Season from the evening of 24 December until 6 January. Generally, however, they lasted longer than the nominal 'twelve days of Christmas' and were associated in particular with Twelfth Night, the evening of 5 January. (Epiphany, 6 January, marked the end of Christmastide: *distyll y gwyliau*, 'the ebb of the holidays'). All three customs have disappeared in their primitive form, but the *Mari Lwyd* is still occasionally performed in Glamorgan – Llangynwyd and Cardiff in particular – and in a few other parts of Wales.

The *Mari Lwyd* was the name given to a horse's skull decorated with coloured ribbons. Bottle glass was used to represent the eyes, and pieces of black cloth to represent the ears. A pole was inserted into the horse's skull and covered with a white sheet. The man carrying the pole crouched beneath the sheet and operated the jaw, while a party of men led the *Mari* from house to house during the hours of darkness. In Glamorgan, according to the Rev. William Roberts, 'Nefydd' (*Crefydd yr Oesoedd Tywyll*, 1852, p.15), the party consisted of the man carrying the horse's skull, the 'Leader', 'Sergeant', 'Merryman' and 'Punch and Judy'. The Merryman would sometimes play the fiddle, and Punch and Judy would wear tattered clothes and had blackened faces, Judy (Siwan) carried a broom.

As the party approached the door traditional and extempore verses were sung to ask for admittance. One of the most popular songs in Glamorgan opened with the following familiar verse:

> *Wel, dyma ni'n dwad*
> *Gyfeillion diniwad*
> *I 'mofyn am gennad i ganu.*
> ('Behold here we come, simple friends, to ask for permission to sing.')

The people inside the house also replied in verse and pretended to refuse entry. A contest in impromptu verse followed until eventually the callers were allowed into the house. Once inside, the *Mari* chased the young women folk, the Merryman with his fiddle performed tricks, and Judy pretended to clean the hearth with her broom. When the dancing, singing and horse-play was over the party was given food and drink. On leaving they again sang to wish the family health and happiness throughout the year.

The Welsh word *Mari* may be a form of the English 'mare', a female horse, or 'mare' as in 'nightmare': a female monster. *Lwyd* means 'grey'. Another suggestion is that *Mari* is equated with the Virgin Mary and *Lwyd*, therefore, would mean 'holy'.

Wassailing

The *Mari Lwyd* ceremony may be a variant of the age-old custom of wassailing 'in which a horse-cult element was incorporated, possibly under the guise of Mary-ritual'. Traditional and impromptu verses were also sung by the wassail party. The revellers, calling at their neighbours' houses, carried with them a beautiful ornamental wassail bowl with looped handles. Once inside the house the family would fill the bowl with warm beer, spices and sometimes baked apples. The bowl was then passed from one person to the other, and dancing and further refreshments followed the ritual drinking. On departing the callers sang to wish the family health, fertile crops and increased livestock. The custom of wassailing was associated with Christmas, the New Year, Twelfth Night, the Feast of Mary of the Candles (2 February) and May Day.

The wassail bowl illustration on the map is based on a bowl made by Thomas Arthyr Deber, Ewenni, Glamorgan, in 1834. The cover is ornamented with loops and moulded figures of animals and birds. On the lower part of the bowl there is an imperfect *englyn* (a verse in the strict *cynghanedd* metre).

Hunting the Wren

Edward Lhuyd (1660–1709) in his *Parochialia* has given us an early description in Welsh of the ancient international custom of Hunting the Wren.

> *They are accustomed in Pembrokeshire, etc. to carry a wren on a bier on Twelfth Night; from a young man to his sweetheart, that is two or three bear it in a bier (covered) with ribbons, and sing carols. They also go to other houses where there are no sweethearts and there will be beer, etc.*

A number of songs attest to the popularity of the custom in various parts of Wales, but particularly in Pembrokeshire where it was practised up to the end of the nineteenth century.

Sometimes a sparrow would be used if a wren could not be caught. It is believed that the original purpose of the custom was to sacrifice the wren in order to ensure the fertility of land and livestock. Later, and especially during the Roman Saturnalia, festival of light, the wren was considered king of all the birds and occupied an important place in the celebration of Christmas and the New Year in many countries.

The wooden wren-house, decorated with coloured ribbons, illustrated on the map, was made in 1869 by Richard Cobb, sexton, Marloes, Pembrokeshire.

Love spoons

Wooden spoons carved by young men and presented to their sweethearts as tokens of affection were very popular in Wales from the seventeenth to the nineteenth centuries. The earliest surviving example in St Fagans' collection is dated 1667, but the custom was in all probability widespread in Wales before that date.

Carving of spoons for domestic use was an age-old craft, and it is possible that the first wooden spoons given as tokens were also used by the recipient for eating. 'However, once the utilitarian function of the love-spoon was discarded, there was no limit to the variations which could be introduced in size, shape and decoration. Since the donor made the gift himself he sought to emphasize the feeling and care which had gone into its making by elaborating the technique and departing from the useful and functional original.' Symbols carved on intricately decorated spoons include hearts, anchors, key-holes, small wooden loose balls, chains, birds, vines and wheels.

May Dancing

Our ancestors divided the year into two dominant seasons: summer and winter. May Day was known as *Calan Haf*, 'the calend of summer', and the first of November as *Calan Gaeaf*, 'the winter calend'. As May Day marked the beginning of summer in the old Celtic calendar, it was time for celebration, festivities and customs, associated in particular with courtship, the open air and the regeneration of nature. *Dawnsio Haf*, 'May or summer dancing' and the May-pole custom (often in conjunction with Morris dancing or *Dawns y Fedwen*, 'the dance of the birch') was once a well known activity throughout Wales. In South Wales the May-pole custom was called *Codi'r Fedwen*, 'raising the birch', and in the North *Y Gangen Haf*, 'the summer branch'.

The illustration on the map depicts a version of the May-pole dance, mainly associated with North East Wales, in which the May-pole proper has been replaced by a decorated garland. The garland (according to H.T.B., a correspondent of William Hone's *Every-Day Book*, vol. 1, 1825, cols. 562–5, quoted in *Welsh Folk Customs*, pp. 104–5) consisted of

> *a long staff or pole with a triangular or square frame attached to it. The frame was covered with strong white linen and the silver spoons were fixed on it in the shape of stars, squares or circles. Between these were rows of watches; and at the top of the frame opposite the pole in its centre, the collection was crowned by the largest of the ornaments borrowed – usually a silver cup or tankard. The decorated garland was left over May-eve at the farmhouse from whence the most liberal loan of silver had been received, or with a farmer known to all as a good master and liberal to the poor; its deposit was a token of respect.*

The garland was carried by the chief character in the May Dancing party, namely the *Cadi* or the Fool.

> *His dress was partly male, partly female: a coat and waistcoat for the upper part of the body, and petticoats for the lower part. He wore a hideous mask, or else his face was blackened and his lips, cheeks and the orbits of his eyes painted red.*

All the other dancers wore dresses decorated with the most colourful ribbons available and would dance before each farmhouse visited. The *Cadi* played the clown and collected money from the household, 'thanking them with bows and curtsies'.

Y Gaseg Fedi: 'The Harvest Mare'

The successful garnering of the harvest was an occasion for celebration and rejoicing. One of the most popular customs – in West Wales in particular – was *Y Gaseg Fedi*, 'The Harvest Mare', a name for the last sheaf of corn to be harvested. It was also called *y gaseg ben fedi*, 'the-end-of-the-reaping-mare'. In Pembrokeshire it was called *gwrach*, 'hag'.

To celebrate the end of the harvest the last tuft in the field was left standing, and the head-servant plaited it with care and skill, as evidenced by the illustration on the map. There then followed a contest among the farmworkers to cut the sheaf with their reaping-hooks, each worker standing a certain distance from the 'mare'. The head-servant would be the first contestant.

The successful reaper then shouted a traditional rhyme. In Carmarthenshire the last line of the rigmarole was: *Pen medi bach mi ces hi* ('I've got a little harvest mare'). His task then – indeed his feat – was to carry the 'mare' into the farmhouse and hang it dry on a beam in the kitchen. The women folk would drench him with water and other liquids to try and wet the 'mare'. If the bearer was successful in carrying the 'mare' into the house dry he would be given a place of honour at the table during the harvest feast and he could command as much beer as he wanted. If he failed, he would be an object of derision. The 'mare' was kept in the house until the next harvest as a decoration and, in some districts, as a protective charm. In Eastern parts of Wales in particular the corn decorations were more finely plaited and purely ornamental (as the two examples in the illustration show).

Variations of the Harvest Mare custom exist in other parts of Europe and, as Sir James Fraser in *The Golden Bough* has suggested, they probably reflect the ancient belief that the corn-spirit and the forces of natural growth remained potent in the last sheaf of the harvest.

Bibliography

General

Aarne, Antti and Stith Thompson, *The Types of the Folktale. A Classification and Bibliography*, Folklore Fellows Communications (F.F.C.), 2nd revised edition, Helsinki, 1961.

Briggs, Katharine M., *A Dictionary of British Folk-Tales in the English Language*, part A, vols. 1–2, part B, vols. 1–2, Routledge and Kegan Paul, London, 1970–1.

Christiansen, Reidar Th., *The Migratory Legends. A Proposed List of Types with a Systematic Catalogue of the Norwegian Variants*, F.F.C., no. 175, Helsinki, 1958.

Dégh, Linda, *Folktales and Society. Story-Telling in a Hungarian Peasant Community*, Indiana University Press, Bloomington, 1969.

Dorson, Richard M., general editor of the series: 'The Folktales of the World', Routledge and Kegan Paul and Chicago University Press, London and Chicago, 1963–

Dundes, Alan, *The Study of Folklore*, Prentice-Hall, Englewood Cliffs, N.J., 1965.

Folklore. Journal of The English Folklore Society, 1878–

Fabula. Journal of Folktale Studies, Berlin and New York, 1957.

Ranke, Kurt, ed., *European Anecdotes and Jests*, Rosenkilde and Bagger, Copenhagen, 1972.

Thompson, Stith, *The Folktale*, The Dryden Press, New York, 1946.

Thompson, Stith, *Motif-Index of Folk Literature*, vols. 1–6, revised edition, Rosenkilde and Bagger, Copenhagen, 1955.

Williams, J. E. Caerwyn, *Y Storïwr Gwyddeleg a'i Chwedlau*, Gwasg Prifysgol Cymru (G.P.C.), Caerdydd, 1972.

Wales

Bromwich, Rachel, *Trioedd Ynys Prydein. The Welsh Triads*, University of Wales Press (U.W.P.), Cardiff, 1961.

Davies, Elwyn, gol./ed., *Rhestr o Enwau Lleoedd. A Gazetteer of Welsh Place-Names*, G.P.C./ U.W.P., Caerdydd/Cardiff, 1967.

Davies, Jonathan Ceredig, *Folk-Lore of West and Mid-Wales*, the author, Aberystwyth, 1911.

Davies, Sioned, *Crefft y Cyfarwydd. Astudiaeth o Dechnegau Naratif yn y Mabinogion* ('a study of the narrative techniques in the Mabinogion'), U.W.P., Cardiff, 1995

Davies, Sioned, *The Mabinogion. Translated with an Introduction and Notes*, Oxford University Press, 2007.

Evans, Hugh, *Y Tylwyth Teg*, Gwasg y Brython, Lerpwl, 1935.

Evans, Myra, *Casgliad o Chwedlau Newydd*, Cambrian News, Aberystwyth [1926].

Foulkes, Isaac, gol., *Cymru Fu…*, Hughes a'i Fab, Wrecsam, 1862.

Gruffydd, Eirlys, *Gwrachod Cymru*, Gwasg Gwynedd, Caernarfon, 1980.

Gwyndaf, Robin, *Storïau Gwerin Cymru*, cyfres Casetiau Amgueddfa Werin Cymru, rhif 1, Caerdydd, 1976.

Gwyndaf, Robin, *The Welsh Folk Narrative Tradition: Adaptation and Continuity*, reprinted from *Folk Life*, vol. 26, 1987–8, National Museum of Wales (Welsh Folk Museum).

Gwyndaf, Robin, *Straeon Gwerin Cymru*, cyfres Llyfrau Llafar Gwlad, rhif 10, Gwasg Carreg Gwalch, Capel Garmon, 1988.

Gwyndaf, Robin, *Tales of Welsh Tradition-Bearers*. Texts in Welsh, with an English tranlsation and a sound recording, of 32 folk tales; National Museum of Wales: www.welshfolktales.org

Humphreys, Emyr, *The Taliesin Tradition: A Quest for the Welsh Identity*, Black Raven Press, London, 1983.

Huws, John Owen, *Y Tylwyth Teg*, Llyfrau Llafar Gwlad, rhif 4, 1987.

Huws, John Owen, *Casglu Straeon Gwerin yn Eryri*, Llyfrau Llafar Gwlad, rhif 170, Gwasg Carreg Gwalch, Llanrwst, 2008

Huws, John Owen, *Straeon Gwerin Ardal Eryri*, vols 1 a 2, Gwasg Carreg Gwalch, 2008.

Ifans, Dafydd a Rhiannon, *Y Mabinogion*, diweddariad, ynghyd â rhagymadrodd gan Brynley F. Roberts, Gwasg Gomer, Llandysul, 1980.

Isaac, Evan, *Coelion Cymru*, Gwasg Aberystwyth, 1938.

Jarman, A. O. H., gol., *Chwedlau Cymraeg Canol*, G.P.C., ail arg., 1969.

Jarman, A. O. H., *The Legend of Merlin*, U.W.P., 1960,

Jones, Bedwyr Lewis, *Arthur y Cymry. The Welsh Arthur*, G.P.C./U.W.P., 1975.

Jones, Gwyn a Thomas, *The Mabinogion*, J. M. Dent, Everyman edition, London, 1948.

Jones, J. (Myrddin Fardd), *Llên Gwerin Sir Gaernarfon*, Cwmni y Cyhoeddwyr Cymreig, Caernarfon, 1908.

Jones, Thomas, 'Y Stori Werin yng Nghymru', *Trafodion Cymdeithas Anrhydeddus y Cymmrodorion*, tymor 1970, rhan 1, tt. 16–32.

Jones, T. Gwynn, *Welsh Folklore and Folk-Custom*, Methuen, Llundain, 1930. (Reprinted with a new introduction and bibliography by Arthur ap Gwynn; D. S. Brewer, Woodbridge and Totowa, 1979.) An excellent introduction to Welsh folklore.

Lhuyd, Edward, *Parochialia…*, supplement to *Archaeologia Cambrensis*, vols. 9–11, 6th series, 1909–11.

Llafar Gwlad, cylchgrawn Cymdeithas Llafar Gwlad, 1983–

Owen, Elias, *Welsh Folk-lore: A collection of the Folk-tales and Legends of North Wales*, Woodall and Minshall, Oswestry and Wrexham, 1896. (E.P. Publishing, 1976).

Owen, Trefor M., *Welsh Folk Customs*, National Museum of Wales (Welsh Folk Museum), Cardiff, 1959.

Owen, Trefor M., *The Customs and Traditions of Wales*. Second edition, with an introduction by Emma Lile, U.W.P., 2016.

Parry, Thomas, *A History of Welsh Literature*, translated by H. Idris Bell, The Clarendon Press, Oxford, 1955.

Parry-Jones, D., *Welsh Legends and Fairy Lore*, illustrated by Ifor Owen, Batsford, London, 1953.

Rees, Alwyn and Brynley, *Celtic Heritage. Ancient Tradition in Ireland and Wales*, Thames and Hudson, London, 1961.

Rhŷs, John, *Celtic Folklore: Welsh and Manx*, vols. 1–2, The Clarendon Press, Oxford, 1901. (Wildwood House, 1980).

Sikes, Wirt, *British Goblins: Welsh Folk-lore, Fairy Mythology, Legends and Traditions*, Sampson Law, London, 1880. (E.P. Publishing, 1973).

Stephens, Meic, gol./ed., *Cydymaith i Lenyddiaeth Cymru*, G.P.C., 1986. *The Oxford Companion to the Literature of Wales*, Oxford University Press, 1986.

Trevelyan, Marie, *Folk-Lore and Folk Stories of Wales*, Elliot Stock, London, 1909.

Thomas, Gwyn, *Y Mabinogi*, darluniwyd gan Margaret Jones, G.P.C., ar ran Cyngor Celfyddydau Cymru, 1984. An English translation was published by Gwyn Thomas and Kevin Crossley-Holland, *Tales from the Mabinogion*, illustrated by Margaret Jones, Victor Gollancz, London, 1984.

Thomas, Gwyn, *Culhwch ac Olwen*, darluniwyd gan Margaret Jones, G.P.C., ar ran Cyngor Celfyddydau Cymru, 1988. An English version was published by Gwyn Thomas and Kevin Crossley-Holland, *The Quest for Olwen*, illustrated by Margaret Jones, Lutterworth Press, Cambridge, 1988.

Williams, Ifor, *Hen Chwedlau*, G.P.C., 1949.

Williams, Ifor, *Chwedl Taliesin*, G.P.C., 1957.

Yates, Dora E., ed., *XXI Welsh Gypsy Folk-Tales*, collected by John Sampson, Gregynog Press, Newtown, 1933. (Robinson Publishing, 1984).

Margaret Jones with the author, at the launch of her beautiful volume, *The Revelation of John*, at the National Library of Wales, 11 October 2008. The volume was edited and published by Robin Gwyndaf (August, 2008).

Photo courtesy of Arwyn Parry-Jones.

Also available from Y Lolfa

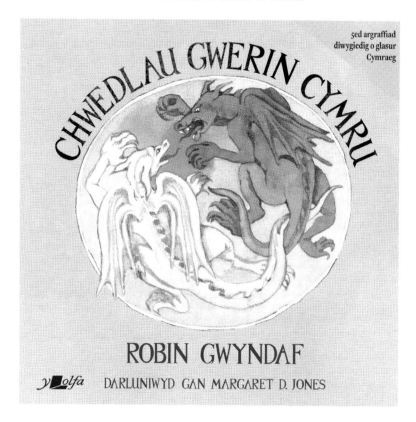

£9.99

Ar gael hefyd yr un pryd â'r ddwy gyfrol Gymraeg a Saesneg, y mae map hardd o Gymru, ar ffurf poster: *Chwedlau Gwerin Cymru: Welsh Folk Tales*. Yr ymchwil a'r dylunio gan Robin Gwyndaf, a'r arlunwaith gan Margaret D. Jones.

Also available to accompany the two Welsh and English versions of the book is a beautiful map of Wales, in the form of a poster: Chwedlau Gwerin Cymru: Welsh Folk Tales. *Research and design by Robin Gwyndaf; illustrated by Margaret D. Jones.*

CHWEDLAU GWERIN CYMRU
WELSH FOLK TALES

Ymchwil a dylunio / Research and design: Robin Gwyndaf
Darlun / illustration: Margaret D Jones